THE
CAPTIVE

CH

THE
CAPTIVE

JOYCE HANSEN

**SCHOLASTIC
HARDCOVER**

Scholastic Inc.
New York

With special thanks to Joanne Edey-Rhodes, Lecturer, Department of Black and Puerto Rican Studies, Hunter College; and to Dr. Joyce Toney, Associate Professor, Department of Black and Puerto Rican Studies, Hunter College, for fact-checking the manuscript.

Library of Congress Cataloging-in-Publication Data available
Library of Congress number: 93-083134
ISBN 0-590-41625-1

12 11 10 9 8 7 6 5 4 3 2 1   3 4 5 6 7 8/9

Printed in the U.S.A.   37

First Scholastic printing, January 1994

For Matt

Contents

Prologue   ix

I. Journey to Kumasi   1

II. The Golden Stool   9

III. Betrayal   18

IV. Captured   25

V. Kofi's Song   36

VI. The Search   44

VII. Escape   52

VIII. The Coast   67

IX. The Slaver   75

X. Friends   81

XI. Bought and Sold   93

XII. A Strange New World   102

XIII. A New Home   114

XIV. The Long House   120

XV. Secret Lessons   128

XVI. Plans   137

XVII. Decisions   144

XVIII. Runaways   158

XIX. The Captain   166

XX. The Hearing   175

XXI. A Face from the Past   186

Epilogue   193

Author's Note   194

Prologue

Sierra Leone
West Africa
March 1811

My name is *Kofi Kwame Paul and I am the first mate on the brig,* **The Traveller.** *Kofi was the name given to me by my family, for I was born on a Friday. The other two names I claimed for myself —Kwame after my natural father and Paul for the man who gave me a second life, the captain of* **The Traveller,** *Paul Cuffe.*

As I gaze at the dark sand on the shores of Sierra Leone, a British colony in Africa, I cannot help but recall the extraordinary circumstances of my life that took me far from my African village to a New England village and now back again to Africa.

Once again I will feel the sun and breathe in the air of the continent that gave me birth. Memories of Africa pull me to the past as **The Traveller** *sails forward.*

I
Journey to Kumasi

Ashanti Kingdom
West Africa
1788

I was twelve seasons old when my life changed forever. Our entire clan was going to Kumasi for the annual ceremony in honor of the Ashanti kings past and present, one of our most important celebrations.

All of the wives, children, uncles, aunts, and elders of our clan made the trek to the city of Kumasi. Many other families also traveled with us — over a hundred people from my village. We were all a part of the great Ashanti kingdom.

I was the youngest of my father and mother's five children. My father, Kwame, had other wives and children, for he was a great chief, but my mother always told us that we, Kwesi, Manu, Intim, Afua, and I, were his favorites.

I laughed and played with my friends and cousins as we walked along a narrow path framed by the wide branches of the cedar trees that formed a green, leafy ceiling. Narrow shafts of sunlight lit our path.

"Kofi!" my father's stern voice silenced me.

"You linger and joke as if we were safe in our own compound. Hurry along."

I scurried behind him. Why did it matter that we were not home? As long as he and my brothers were there, we were all safe.

The other children ran back to their families, and I threw my head up proudly as if I were already a famous chief like Kwame. Someday, I, too, would be a great chief, but at that moment I only wanted to wrestle, throw javelins, and romp with my friends.

"You should be with your mother and the other women and children," Manu, my eldest brother, teased. If my father and my other brothers, Intim and Kwesi, weren't there I would not have let Manu talk to me in such a way. I wasn't a child anymore. I was old enough to carry my father's stool when we presented ourselves to the king.

Being Kwame's stool bearer was the main reason for my excitement. Every important chief and official had a stool symbolizing his power and authority. It was an honor to carry it. And I, Kofi, my father's youngest son, was given that honor. I changed my face into a serious mask and tried to concentrate only on my brothers' and father's talk. But as usual they spoke of trading and the foreigners from across the ocean.

"The Fantis are growing powerful under the British," Manu said.

"They will never be as powerful as we are," my father replied, practically closing his eyes as he always did when he was thinking deeply about things. Intim narrowed his dark eyes. "So much kidnapping and unlawful slavery," he grumbled as he stepped around a fallen log.

"People are making war just to get slaves to sell to the white men. Caravans leave for the coast every day." Kwesi spoke as deep worry lines creased his forehead. "The trouble always stems from the coast. The white traders want more and more slaves. The chiefs and kings want more and more guns." He slowed his pace and gazed at the red soil. "One day the sons of kings and chiefs will be made slaves."

Manu smiled. "Kwesi, you feel a breeze and think it's a storm. It will never come to that."

It was hard for me to listen to their discussion in my joyous mood. Glancing at a bird with brilliant yellow feathers flapping and cawing through a green wall of leaves, I wanted to screech and flap over everyone's head, too. This was no time to talk about kidnappings and other miseries.

The women nervously urged the older children to hurry and not wander away, and I also began to feel tense. Were we really in danger? Who would dare to hurt us? Why did we have to rush? We had one whole day to reach Kumasi. There should be enough time to stop and rest more

3

often and to watch the birds dance from tree to tree. Only the babies seemed calm — sleeping on their mothers' backs.

My brothers and father continued to talk. Behind me, the voice of my sister, Afua, rose above the conversations of my mother and the other women. She would be getting married when we returned to our home. I knew that she was talking of her pending marriage ceremony, since lately she spoke of nothing else.

I shaded my eyes from the sun's glare when we entered a clearing and saw Oppong, tall and straight, carrying my father's important belongings. I preferred being with him more than listening to my brothers' conversation. If anyone knew what was happening it would be Oppong, my father's slave. He'd lived with us before I was even born and was a member of our family. Father was allowing him to marry Afua.

Oppong had taught me how to play the flute and how to turn a block of wood into the figure of a man or a woman. He taught me the language of birds and other living creatures. And he taught me how to understand the messages contained in the colors of the sky and the soil and the smell and touch of a breeze.

I ran over to him. "Why is my father so worried?" I asked. "Can we be attacked on our way to Kumasi?"

He flinched as if I'd discovered a secret. "Don't

4

talk foolishness." He waved me away impatiently. "No one would dare attack a powerful man like your father. He's only anxious to get to the ceremony. Take out your flute and play some music to pass the time, Kofi."

I always felt safe and secure around Oppong. Why did he seem disturbed? He should be happy. Our great day of celebration was near, and soon he'd be a member of our clan.

Reaching into my leather bundle, I took my flute out and immediately forgot Oppong's strangeness as I made my music.

"Now," Oppong said, "you possess time and can make it pass as quickly or as slowly as you want it to." My rhythms were as quick as the birds flitting from branch to branch.

"Oh, Kofi, Oppong has taught you well," a woman from my village exclaimed. My grandmother agreed.

Afua began to make up words to go along with the tune I created, and I imagined that everyone who heard my flute grew happy and that mothers no longer nervously called their children.

We walked for a long time, and just as dusk began to fall, the forest gradually disappeared into cultivated yam fields. It was about another mile before we reached the outskirts of Kumasi. The red walls of the guest compounds where we would stay were a welcomed sight. Some of the residents of the city greeted us with food.

We remained outside of Kumasi through the next day, since it was a Friday and there could be no traveling the day before the ceremony on Saturday. We children were mad with excitement and got in everyone's way. I decided to find Oppong, knowing that he would be happy to see me.

A bright sun shone on groups of men repairing their state umbrellas — large enough to cover several people. The girls and young women braided and adorned their hair with beads and cowrie shells. Some women fed their babies; others pounded the cornmeal that would be used to make fou-fou.

I looked for Oppong among a group of young men his age who were mending umbrellas.

"Have you seen Oppong?" I asked.

"No," one of them answered. "Not since early this morning."

Where was he, I wondered. He should be busy preparing for tomorrow. Maybe he was with my father or one of my brothers, I thought. Just as I started to look for my father, Oppong walked through the gates of the compound. I dashed over to him. "Oppong, where have you been?"

"Come, help me with my chores. There's much to do."

"I know," I said, trotting quickly to keep up with his long strides. "That's why I was wondering why I couldn't find you."

He ignored me and hurried quickly toward my father's guest hut.

Kwame wasn't there but was with the other elders and chiefs. It was a good thing, too, for he would have been angry with Oppong for staying away all morning. I was curious and wished he had taken me. "Did you go to Kumasi? What did you see?"

"Come, come," he said sternly, "we have a lot to do."

What was wrong with my good friend, I wondered. While Oppong sewed a tear in my father's official state umbrella, I polished the carved posts of Kwame's wooden stool.

In the evening we all listened to one of the elder's recount the history of our people. The thin old man, dressed in a white robe, closed his eyes as he spoke. "Our first king was Chu Mientwi, followed by Kobina Amamfi. Our next great king, Oti Akentin, had an army of sixty thousand brave men to defend our mighty kingdom. During the reign of our next king, Obiri Yeboa Manu . . ." The elder talked at length as I listened with rapt attention. I remained awake until he finished, for I loved to hear the history of our people. I imagined that one day I, too, could be a great king who made a happy life for all of his subjects.

Before we slept that night, our priest reminded us of the sacredness of the next day's ceremony. "We will appease the spirits of our kings who have passed on to the other side, and we will ask for the purification of our nation. We ask that evil not find us and that the new year comes in peace."

As I lay down on my mat, I realized that Oppong had not been with us during the elder's talk. But I thought no more about his absence as I fell off into a deep and peaceful sleep.

II
The Golden Stool

The next morning, after bathing in the bath hut and eating a filling breakfast of porridge, I went back to the hut I'd slept in with the other young males in our group. I put on the new robe my father had given me, woven in burgundy, blue, and yellow patterns. Like most boys my age, I usually wore a simple white cloth around my hips; however, since I was the son of an important chief and a distant member of the royal family and since this was an important occasion, I would wear a new robe.

Everyone wore special robes. Brilliant hues of blue, yellow, green, white, violet, red, and sienna paraded before me as I left the hut and went to find my mother. She sat outside of the guest compound with my sister, Afua. I proudly showed myself off to them. "You outshine the sun, Kofi," Afua said, fingering a section of the robe thrown over my shoulders. The copper bracelets that encircled her bare brown arms tinkled as she moved.

Mother touched my face with her soft hands. "See my handsome son. You have your father's and his father's round eyes and face, and skin the color of the red-brown earth — the kind that produces the best yams." She threw her head back, and her laugh was as bright as her copper earrings, glinting light back at the sun.

I then searched for Oppong to show him my robe. I didn't see him among the groups of young men and remembered that he had not been with us the night before. A hawk's cry drew my gaze toward a nearby knoll softly rising above the fields. "Oppong!" I shouted as he walked toward me. I thought that I saw several men slip quickly into the forest, but I wasn't certain. Maybe the morning light and lingering shadows of the night were playing tricks on me.

I rushed to his side. "I saw some people going into the forest. Who are they? Why aren't you wearing the new robe Afua gave you?"

"Sh-h-h-h," he ordered. "You must have imagined you saw someone, just as I did. That's why I went to investigate." He adjusted his sword. "If anyone was there, I didn't want to be seen. It's hard to hide in a bright robe." Oppong smiled admiringly at me. "You are a fine-looking prince," he said.

"My dear father gave it to me." I twirled and preened in my robe until Oppong stopped me. Leaning slightly in the direction of the forest, his body stiffened, and he became as still and silent as a rock.

"If you think you see something," I whispered sharply, "why don't you tell the guards?"

Oppong put his arms around my shoulders. "You have much to learn. Suppose we are outnumbered? You must check your enemy's strength, so you know whether to attack or run."

We walked slowly toward the groups of people. Some had finally started to move on.

"I thought I saw something, too," I whispered, looking back toward the forest.

Oppong turned my head forward. "Don't worry yourself," he said. "Come, Kofi, I have to finish cleaning your father's umbrella and help him prepare to leave."

Mothers gathered their children. Servants picked up the official stools, and young boys carefully held the closed umbrellas that would be used in the procession into Kumasi.

I heard my father calling me from inside the hut where he'd slept, and I hurried to him. Sitting on a goatskin mat, he motioned for me to sit before him.

"Kofi, you are my father come back to this world. You have his face. You are becoming a man, and as you know you'll have the honor of carrying my stool in the procession." He reached into a small basket at his side. "This is for you." He handed me a newly carved flute engraved with a replica of his father's stool. "This was made by one of our master carvers," he said.

I tried not to yelp like a puppy as I ran my fingers along the hard, polished wood. "I'll always keep it with me," I said.

"Here's another gift in honor of this day." He handed me a goldweight cast in the shape of a goat with its long horns sloping backwards. "This weight is called 'had I known that which has passed behind me.' This is to remind you that regretting that which has already occurred is useless. This is also a symbol of the day when you will be able to wear gold." Only goldsmiths and great men like my father were allowed to wear gold ornaments. He put the goldweight inside a small purse and tied the purse around my neck. "Keep it hidden under your robe. There are a lot of poor scamps about stealing while everyone is celebrating."

"Thank you, Father," I stammered, surprised over the special gifts.

"And don't boast to your brothers and sister." That meant that he hadn't given them gifts. My robe could barely contain my bursting chest. He handed me his stool, and I proudly walked into the bright morning, secure in the knowledge that I, Kofi, though the youngest and the least, was my father's favorite child.

We had less than a half-hour's walk to the city. As we entered Kumasi we heard the deep calls of the water drum. The horns, bells, and drums rivaled God's thunder. The processions of chiefs and noblemen, their wives, children, servants, subjects, and slaves all seemed to be under a tremendous roof formed by the many umbrellas held over the heads of the important chiefs and other dignitaries.

The chiefs sat on the shoulders of their servants so that they could wave to the cheering crowds, while the umbrella bearers moved the umbrellas up and down in order to create a breeze. The numerous processions pressed forward to the Place of Cannon, where every important chief and nobleman would be presented to the king.

The strings of many koras played melodies that stirred us all to sing the stories of our nation. I wished that I had two more hands so that I could play my flute and display my father's stool at the same time.

Kwame, sitting on the shoulders of two servants, waved to the crowds. Oppong and my brothers raised and lowered the umbrella over my father's head. Another servant carried me on his shoulders while I held the stool as high as I could stretch my arms.

Young boys waving plumes and feathers danced around the chiefs. The captains belonging to each important chief proclaimed the great deeds of their leader. When we neared the Place of Cannon where the king and queen would receive us, we saw a forest of people. A sweetish smell of roses from the perfumed oil that many of the men and women had rubbed themselves with filled the air.

Girls and women sang and danced praises to the queen. Their braided hair sparkled with colorful beads, white cowrie shells, and the silver bowls they carried on their heads. The splendid turbans of the Moors rose above the crowds like white minarets as they proudly rode their prancing horses.

The gold bracelets one chief wore were so heavy that he had to rest his arm on a boy's head. Musicians, dancing and playing instruments, headed up each individual procession.

When we finally reached the area where the king and queen sat on ebony chairs on a raised platform in the center of a large court, my childish eyes gazed ahead, absorbing every detail of what stood before me. I hardly knew that I was breathing and felt sorry for every human being who was not there with us at that moment. They had no idea how wonderful life was.

As each great chief entered the arena with his entourage and his captain reciting his brave deeds, the royal couple nodded and smiled.

When it was our turn to present ourselves, I stared closely at the king, who sat as still as a carving and only nodded slightly when my father's captain completed the greeting.

The head royal stool bearer stood at the king's side holding the golden stool — the most sacred shrine and symbol of our nation. Two servants stood on either side of the gold-covered stool holding the tremendous gold bells attached to its ends by thongs. Other servants held the state umbrella, made of camel's hair and wool, over the stool. A gold carving of a war horn sat at the very top of the umbrella we called *katamanso* — the cover of the nation.

After my father paid his respects to the king and pledged his allegiance to the nation, he took his place among the other great chiefs. I sat proudly with him and my brother; for the first time I no longer remained with the women and children on the outskirts of the arena. We sat to the right of the king and queen. The other important chiefs were seated on the left. The horn-blowers and drummers sat before the royal couple.

I noticed a group of white men with their Fanti guides also entering the Place of Cannon to pay their respects to the king. Were these the people who were causing problems, I wondered. It was at this same ceremony last year that I saw white men for the first time. I still had not grown used to the fact that all men did not look like us.

I imagined that they were wearing masks — that underneath the white face was a normal black one. Why didn't they wear colorful robes like us, instead of imprisoning their bodies in tight trousers and high, black boots. Their black guides wore the same uncomfortable-looking clothing. The white men greeted the king and then sat down with their guides while the captains of the important chiefs began their discussions of state business. I tried to concentrate like the adults, listening to the captains of the Ashanti army tell how they once again kept the British from coming into the interior. "They must remain at the coast," one of the captains exclaimed.

I tried to concentrate on the discussion as I tucked my flute under my robe, but my mind roamed. I patted my feet to the various rhythms and tunes still played by the musicians outside the arena and began to feel nostalgic for the times when I danced and sang on the outskirts with the other children.

I turned slightly to say something to Oppong, but he wasn't there. "Where's Oppong?" I whispered to Kwesi. He put his fingers to his lips.

"Listen to the talk. You are with men now."

Sighing, I turned completely around and saw Oppong, looking worried and frightened, pushing his way through the crowd. He clutched my father's arm when he reached us.

"Sir, we must leave," he whispered hoarsely to Kwame, his eyes darting back and forth like two black birds.

"What's wrong?" my father asked, leaning toward him.

"I have learned that later today, during the offering of the new yam, there will be trouble."

"What sort of trouble?"

"Where did you hear this, Oppong?" Kwesi interrupted, trying to sound calm.

"From Chief Kobina's bodyguard. There is a planned attack on the great chiefs, sir, and you are a great chief."

"Who would dare attack us?" my father whispered hoarsely. His large round eyes searched Oppong's face intently.

"A group of coastal people, along with the European slavers, Master, are plotting this mischief in order to weaken our kingdom," Oppong exclaimed averting his eyes from my father's stare. My heart pounded like the water drums beating outside of the arena. Why must this trouble come to my father now?

III
Betrayal

Sweat poured down Oppong's face. I held on tightly to Kwame's stool, hoping that Oppong was wrong.

"Chief Kobina's bodyguard swore that what he said is true. Do you see Kobina? He's gone and he was here when we entered. Your people will be safe, but you, Master . . . I fear for your life."

Oppong brushed his large hand across his forehead. "Let me take you to a safe hiding place, and then you can start back home before the celebrations are done."

"He's right father. Kobina was here. I don't see him now. We should leave." Kwesi stood up.

Manu and Intim looked worried.

"We should leave now," Kwesi insisted.

"His story may be true or it may not be, but we cannot take chances with your safety, Father," Intim said firmly.

Manu's voice trembled slightly, but his fists were tightly clenched. "Things are unsettled. That's what I was telling you before." My father lowered his eyelids, the way he always did when he was thinking deeply.

"It's only your father who is in danger. No one else. I know of a hiding place for him," Oppong said as he nervously wiped his face.

Something was awfully wrong. I thought about how strangely Oppong had been acting and was relieved when Kwesi spoke up. "You expect us to let our father go off alone?"

"You'll bring suspicion on yourselves if everyone leaves. No one else in your family is in danger."

"I'll take care of the family," Intim stated. "Manu and Kwesi, you accompany Father."

"I will go, too," I announced.

"You stay with me," Intim said sternly.

Oppong turned to me. "You remain with Intim. Help him watch over the family."

"No," I shook my head. "I want to go with my father." Did Father know about Oppong's odd behavior? I really wanted to tell them, but suppose I falsely accused my friend of wrongdoing. "Please, Father, let me go with you."

He rubbed my face with his rough hands. "You stay and help your brother watch over your mother and the rest of the family. You're carrying my stool and must stay here to represent me and finish the ceremony."

"Oppong has secrets. He's been acting in a strange way," I blurted out.

Oppong looked shocked, but Intim pushed me down angrily on the bench before Oppong could defend himself. "How dare you speak like that? You're only a child."

"But you said I was a man!"

My father turned to me. "Kofi, Oppong is one of us. You mustn't bring suspicion on someone unless you know what you are speaking of."

I stared at Oppong, whose eyes teared as if he were about to cry. "Little Master, I don't think you mean what you say. All of this talk has upset you." He kneeled before me and tenderly rubbed my head. "I love your father like my own father. I am only trying to protect him."

I felt ashamed and confused. Maybe Oppong *was* trying to help. "You told me this morning that no one would dare attack my father."

"Things change." Oppong's voice was hoarse. "Don't you see Kobina isn't here?"

"But the other chiefs are," Manu commented, gazing around the arena.

All of my brothers spoke at once. Suddenly Kwame stood up. "I have decided. I will leave. These are not times to take rumors lightly."

Kwesi began wringing his hands. "We should send the Europeans back across the water and take control of all of the coastal peoples. There's too much warring." He shook his head. "It has gone too far."

Intim put his arms around Kwesi's shoulders.

"We have to protect our father now. We'll worry about the whites later."

"Intim, you and Kofi stay with the rest of the family. Manu and Kwesi and two of the bodyguards will come with me and Oppong," Kwame said. He put his arm around me. "You have to stay, Kofi, because you are my chief stool bearer. As long as you're here, so am I."

They all agreed, and I sadly watched Oppong lead my father, Kwesi, Manu, and the two bodyguards through the crowd. I lost sight of Kwame, but could see the top of Oppong's head. Intim's attention was drawn back to the proceedings, but there was a deep line across his brow and I knew he was worried, too. I was tortured by uneasy feelings when I caught a glimpse of Chief Kobina entering the arena, talking and laughing with some lesser chiefs. He didn't look like a man in hiding to me.

I grabbed Intim's shoulder. "Look, there's Kobina. He's not in hiding. I have to tell Father and the rest of them."

Before Intim could stop me, I put the stool next to him on the bench and rapidly squeezed past the seated men. Intim tried to pull me back, but he tripped. I glanced behind me quickly, and the last image I saw was the king's stool bearer lifting the golden stool over the king's head and my father's stool toppling to the ground.

Pushing as hard as I could through the great

wall of people, I raced out of the arena and blended into the general crowd. I followed in the direction I had seen them walking and was pummeled in the head several times for pushing people out of my way.

Suspecting they'd use the one large street that led from the Place of Cannon directly out of the city, I moved as quickly as I could past the people packed together like sheaves of grass. A Moor, parting the crowd with his horse, rode toward me. As I jumped out of the horse's path, I saw the top of Oppong's head disappearing behind the wall of a compound.

"Father, Oppong, Manu. Wait!" I called, but they couldn't hear me over the drumming and the music.

The compound was small, right on the edge of the forest. This must be the hiding place, I thought, but they raced toward the forest instead, and I followed, holding my precious robe tightly around my legs so as not to tear or dirty it. "Kwesi!" I cried out, but they still didn't hear my useless yelling.

Suddenly, like a swarm of locusts, a group of men attacked them. Oppong had been right. The cowardly bodyguards ran like rabbits. Manu and my father battled two men who were trying to tie them up. A third man already had Kwesi sprawled on the ground and dug his foot in his back.

"Help them! Help them!" I shouted. But I became speechless when I saw one of the same white men who had been at the ceremony standing next to Oppong. Did the white stranger put some powerful magic on Oppong so that he had become as cowardly as my father's guards?

I lunged for the man who fought my father and tried to jump on his back and pull him off Kwame. I heard Kwesi calling me while someone knocked me to the ground. My sandals flew off my feet as I tried to fight against the blows raining down on my head and body. A big, rough hand twisted my arms behind me and quickly bound my wrists and ankles in iron clamps.

Another person covered my mouth with a strip of cloth that muffled my screams and shrieks. I heard shots and saw my father's arms reach for the sky as he fell to the ground where Manu already lay. Twisting my wrists, I tried to free myself and get to Kwame's side. As I jerked my body from side to side, I watched Kwame's still form, his face in the dirt. My pain from the beating was nothing compared to the pain in my heart. My father was dead.

"Why did you shoot him?" Oppong yelled in Ashanti at the white man, who pointed the long firestick at Oppong. The Fanti guide motioned for the man to put the firestick down. "You delivered him to us as we agreed. What did you think we were going to do with this old chief?

Sell him?" He reached inside his trousers and handed Oppong a purse.

Oppong took the purse and without looking back at Kwesi and me disappeared behind the broad trunk of an akata tree. The white man and his Fanti guides also left, walking in the opposite direction as if they were going back to the celebrations. Two men remained with us.

"Stand up!" one of them ordered me and Kwesi, and I could not stop trembling and crying as I stared at the still forms of my father and my brother. Fear, confusion, and hatred gripped me like a monstrous beast with sharp claws. I had been right in suspecting Oppong. But why had no one listened to me? I could only stare at Kwesi, questioning him with my eyes. Why? Why did Oppong betray us?

I looked again at Kwame and Manu and said the prayer for the spirit of the dead. I could not recite them aloud because my mouth was bound. I could only say them in my heart.

IV
Captured

"Move!" the men ordered us. I lost all of my senses and stumbled blindly next to Kwesi. I heard nothing, felt nothing, and thought nothing. I lost all sense of time and do not know how long we walked. The real Kofi was at the ceremony holding his father's throne and playing beautiful songs on his new flute.

We came to the walls of a small compound, and I could hardly stand. Pent up feelings tumbled over me like a violent storm. The image of my father and brother lying on the forest floor with Oppong smiling and taking money from my kidnappers filled me with rage.

When we entered the compound, groups of men and women, hands and feet tied, sat quietly on the ground. A few dwellings were arranged in a circle. This was no real village with children playing and the smell of pungent smoke from many cooking fires. There were no men returning from their farms. There were only empty-eyed prisoners and men with guns. Though our captors were black men, they wore the same kind of tight trousers and high, black boots that the white men I'd seen wore. They pushed us on the ground with the other people. A tall, skinny man with tremendous hands removed the cloths from our mouths and loosened our wrists. Then he took off one of the iron clamps from my ankle, and bound us together. A short, fat man waddled over to us.

"Where did you get these two?" he asked, examining Kwesi and me very closely. I could tell from the way he spoke that he was not an Ashanti.

"The boy has no family or clan to care for him, and the older one is a criminal," one of our captors said. I knew the trick that these two men were trying to play. Under our law, criminals could be enslaved as a punishment for their crimes.

"He's lying," I shouted at the fat man. "They shot our father and brother. We are the sons of the great chief, Kwame."

"Kofi, please," Kwesi tried to hush me.

"Quiet! You are a child. How dare you speak to an adult like that?" he fired back at me and turned to the fat man. "This boy is a scamp, sir."

"The boy is telling the truth," Kwesi said calmly. "We were kidnapped." The liar flew in Kwesi's face.

"You are a criminal," he shouted. "And if

either of you says one more thing, you will be shot."

The fat one waved his hand at the man. "Now who would be so stupid as to shoot what the white man is willing to pay us for?" He felt the hem of my robe. "They are wearing royal robes." He turned to the liar. "I'll give each of you a hide or one musket for them," he said, folding his arms.

"Is that all?"

"If their story is true and I have the great chief's sons, then you've sold me trouble. I could be punished as a criminal myself. Should I trade gold and ivory and good weapons for trouble?" He turned his broad back to them and flung his toga over one shoulder. "Take my offer or keep your slaves."

My lips quivered as angry tears spilled down my face. My gentle brother said, "Kofi, speak no more. Those two men are stupid, which makes them very dangerous. We would do better to be bought by this fat trader. We can make him believe us. Those other two are merely poor rascals who left their farms to get rich in the trade."

I kept quiet and hoped that Kwesi was correct. The fat man's servants returned with the musket, and our kidnappers raised a fuss. "This is junk," the liar said, "an old, inferior thing."

"You've come to me with an inferior story." The trader held the musket in his outstretched hands. "This is what the white man has brought you from his country." The men took the gun and left. The fat trader waddled away, leaving us with the other people.

I turned to Kwesi. "What place is this? And why did Oppong do this to us? Why?" I wailed and vainly tried to pull off the clamps that bound my ankles to Kwesi's.

He placed a trembling hand on my wrist. His voice sounded weak and far away. "Kofi, I am sorry. You tried to warn us. Had we only known and not listened to Oppong, but to you."

I remembered the goldweight in the shape of a goat with its horns turned backward that our father had given me.

"*Nim sa,*" I said, trembling. "Regrets are vain."

Kwesi looked at me with surprise. "Yes, you're right, Kofi. It's no use to regret what has already passed." He looked at me as if he were seeing me in a new way. "In a few hours, Kofi, you have changed from a boy to a man."

A man must know no joy, I thought, for I would never again be happy. "What place is this?" I asked once more.

"Men and women are bought and sold here." His quivering voice was barely audible.

"Why did Oppong do this? Father treated him like a son. He loved Oppong."

Kwesi shook his head and covered his face. "Oppong was a baby when his village was

28

burned down by slave raiders. He was found by Father in the ruins of that remote village — a naked, crying infant. He has no idea of who his family was." Kwesi drew his lips into a thin, hard line and shook his head. "He became a bitter, jealous man, Kofi, who resented his own and his family's misfortune — and our family's fortune.

"But Father saved him."

Kwesi sighed deeply. "That didn't matter, Kofi. Jealousy is like an illness. And so is greed. He got a lot of gold, too, for delivering a powerful man like Father to his enemies."

"Why would anyone want to kill Father?"

His wide eyes seemed to hold all the sorrow of the world. "We are a powerful people who have taken over many nations. We have a lot of enemies. The coastal whites are afraid of our power and are trying to weaken us. What better way to do that than to kill our leaders," he said.

Suddenly I had a terrible thought. "Afua. Suppose Oppong returns and marries her? We have to get back to warn them," I cried, pulling on the clamps again.

Kwesi's sad eyes were beginning to look dazed. "He won't return to our family and is probably on his way to the coast. If he'd wanted to go back with a story about how we'd all been attacked and only he'd escaped, then he would have had us murdered, too."

My head pounded like a thousand drums as I

gazed around at the clusters of chained men and women. A new feeling entered my soul. Hatred. I sobbed and again pulled at the clamps on my ankles. "We have to leave, Kwesi. We have to find Oppong and kill him. Kill him." I rocked back and forth, grasping the irons. Kwesi forced my fingers loose.

"Kofi, Kofi, we do not repay evil with evil. Oppong will be punished for his deeds."

I crumpled sobbing in Kwesi's lap as if he were my mother. I didn't feel like much of a man. Kwesi rubbed my back and let me cry until I was too weak to cry anymore.

I took my goldweight out of the purse. "Kwesi," I whispered, "see what Father gave me."

He looked surprised. "Father gave you that?"

"Yes. Do you think if we show it to that bull of a man, he'll believe our story? We might trade it for our freedom?" I asked.

"We're worth more than a goldweight to him."

I dug under my robe and partially pulled out the flute.

"Look, he also gave me this. I would sell it even though it is the most wonderful thing I possess."

Kwesi rubbed his hand along the hard, smooth wood. "It's beautiful, Kofi. Don't let the guards see. It would only be taken from you, and we still wouldn't be free. That man is going to sell us right away for as much money as he can get. But maybe we can use these things to convince him that we are the sons of a great Ashanti chief."

As daylight turned to dusk, two men walked into the compound, followed by a group of their servants. The last rays of sunlight fell on the blue and orange patterns in their robes, and the gold bracelets circling their wrists were as thick as the iron clamp around my ankles. One of them spoke to the guards, while the other walked over to us.

"Apo, I need five young men to work on my farm," the man shouted to the fat one who was waddling toward us. He glanced at Kwesi.

I loved my brother very much, for we were sons of the same mother, but I wished then that Kwesi were Intim or Manu. They would not sit as quietly and patiently as he. But that was why Manu was dead. I thought about the ceremony and the joy that was stolen from us. My mother and sister and other brother thought that we were safely hidden away with Oppong. My head still throbbed, my mouth was dry and cracked, my stomach ached from hunger and fear, but I was a great chief's son and I had to speak out!

"Sir!" I called to the fat man named Apo. He stopped walking and looked around. Kwesi whispered, "Kofi, what are you doing?"

I ignored my brother. "Sir!" I called again.

"Oh," Apo stared at me.

"Sir, my brother and I were kidnapped. We are the sons of Chief Kwame. Who was . . . who

31

was . . ." My bravery was leaving me as Apo continued to stare.

"My father was killed by a man named Oppong!"

Apo grabbed both me and Kwesi by the arms. "You are lying. You were probably this great chief's slaves."

"The boy isn't lying," Kwesi said.

I pulled my goldweight and my flute out of my robe. "My father gave these to me. I was his chief stool bearer at the Odwira ceremony today."

The man who had asked for workers blew on his fingers as if he'd burned himself. "Apo, if he is telling the truth then the Ashantis will surely be paying you a royal visit." He laughed at the trader.

Beads of sweat popped out on Apo's fat face as he fingered the flute. His nervousness made me bold. "If you return us to our home, our people will reward you well, sir. I will tell them how you saved us."

Apo threw his hands in the air. "I should not have bought you from those two scoundrels." He turned to the other man. "Atta, I don't know whether they're lying, but that flute and goldweight are Ashanti." He examined me and Kwesi again. "If you are who you say, then I'll be blamed for your troubles."

"If you return us to our family, you will be rewarded." Kwesi's voice began to fade. "We were betrayed by our slave, Oppong. Our people must be told."

"Please help us," I added.

Apo rubbed his hands together nervously. "If you are telling the truth, then I don't want to be blamed for buying you."

"Sir, we will only tell our people that you saved us," I said.

The other man, Atta, studied us closely. "Their robes are torn and dirty, but they are finely woven. They have smooth healthy skin." Atta then rested his hand on Apo's shoulders. "I think that I believe them."

"They might be tricking me," Apo said. "But listen, Atta, I have an idea. You return the younger one to his family. If his story is true, then they can come and get the older brother. He will be well treated. And I'll give you a fair share of the reward."

Atta was silent a moment. "No. I don't want to be involved with this. Let them go."

"But suppose they're trying to trick me. I gave up a good musket for them." He rubbed his fat, sweaty face. "And they'll fetch a high price at the coast."

"You're still too greedy to let them go in case there is really a reward. You don't want to miss that Ashanti gold." He sucked his teeth in disgust. "And this slave trading with the white foreigners will be your undoing, Apo."

"Come, we're like brothers, you and I. You know I can't allow myself to be tricked. That is why I am a rich man. You return the child to his family. They will trust you because you're not a trader. Any reward that comes to me, I'll generously share with you."

"I'm not interested in rewards. I'll help you this time, but you should heed my warning. This slave trading with the whites is an awful thing, and you should have no dealings with it." He offered me his hand and helped me up, but spoke to Apo. "You should let them go is what you should do."

"I don't know whether their story is true."

Atta waved his hand in exasperation and then addressed me. "I will see that you are returned to your family and then direct them here to get your brother."

"I want my brother with me," I protested.

Apo immediately started removing the clamps from our legs. "I will take good care of your brother," he assured me.

Kwesi and I rubbed our ankles. "Kofi, we will meet again in our own home. Go with the man."

I didn't move. "Go, Kofi. Don't worry about me. We will be together again." I stood up slowly and took a few steps toward the entrance, but looked back at Kwesi. He motioned for me to continue to walk. I didn't want to leave him.

"Kwesi!" I called out as my eyes filled with tears. "Kwesi, please."

He motioned toward the entrance, "Go, Kofi," he repeated, turning his back to me and burying his face in his upraised knees. Taking one last look at my brother, I stumbled out of the compound.

V
Kofi's Song

It was only a short walk before we reached another village. I paid careful attention to the route we took so that I would remember how to get back to Kwesi. The sweetish smell of wood smoke reminded me of my own home. To keep myself from crying I thought of Oppong and how much I hated him. It was easier to think of those I hated than to remember those I loved.

We entered a large compound. Children laughed as they played in the open area of one of the houses. A bright, full moon lit the compound as if it were daylight, and a group of girls sat talking under a large tree. This was not a slave pen, but a real village. It reminded me of my own home and I thought about my mother and sister and Kwame and Manu. I was frightened and alone, without anyone to comfort me. Suppose this man, Atta, was treacherous like Oppong and didn't mean to help me, but planned to sell me at the coast for a high price.

My fears were soon eased. When the men were

sent to the large bath hut outside of the compound, Atta told me to remain with him in his compound and called his wife, Ajoa. She was a tall, graceful woman. Her small bright eyes reminded me of my mother. "He will stay with us until I can return him to his family."

She smiled at me kindly. "What a handsome boy," she said. I felt comfortable with her and told her my story quickly as she led me to the small bath hut attached to her house. "I know of your father," she said. "He was a good and just man who helped his people."

Ajoa left and I squatted in front of a basin filled with water and washed myself. A servant brought me a clean cloth to wrap around my hips. I tied the goldweight around my waist and held the flute tightly as I followed the servant to the woman's home.

Sitting on goatskin mats, we ate a tasty meal of vegetable soup. It was the first decent food I'd had since I'd been kidnapped. Ajoa spotted my flute resting next to me and picked it up. "It's beautiful."

"My father had it made for me."

"Play for me, Kofi."

She closed her eyes as I played a song that was my own and expressed the sadness in my heart. When I finished she opened her eyes and looked at me. "You are like a little bird, Kofi."

Exhausted, I slept a deep but troubled sleep in

a small hut with Ajoa and Atta's sons. When I woke up the next morning, for a moment I thought that I was in my own home. And then I remembered all that had happened the day before and I did not want to open my eyes. Poor Kwesi. I prayed that he was faring well with the fat, greedy trader.

I twisted around on the mat where I lay to make sure that my goldweight was still in my purse and my flute was by my side. They were all that I had left of my father. I couldn't lose them. One of the boys sleeping in the hut was Ajoa's eldest son. He was a few years older than I. "Come, my mother has the morning meal for us," he said as he rummaged through a huge basket near his mat. "You are supposed to be a famous chief's son?"

"Yes," I said, not liking the way he eyed me suspiciously.

"I think your father doesn't even own one yam field," he said and left the hut. The other boys had already gone. I didn't care what he thought. I dismissed him as a foolish boy and took off for the bath hut to wash myself before I ate the morning meal.

The compound, larger than I'd first imagined, was already busy with the morning's activities. Children sat outside their homes eating porridge. Six houses were arranged around a big square. Each house had three walls, and the fourth side of every house opened onto the square. A forked post stood outside of the largest house. A bowl with offerings to the great sky god Nyame rested on top of the post.

A young girl carrying porridge and tea entered the big house in the center. A small stool house where the owner kept his religious articles was attached to the larger house. My father's house was made the same way. That had to be Atta's house, and the girl was, most likely, one of his daughters.

If he had wives beside Ajoa or married sons with wives, the other houses probably belonged to them. There were barns stacked with yams and a shed for the goats and sheep. The cook prepared breakfast in the middle of the compound. Atta was a rich man.

I spotted Atta's sons standing with the men Atta had hired. They were all going to work on his farm. I tried to decide which house was Ajoa's. She called me from the courtyard. As I entered her home, she beckoned me to sit next to her and handed me a bowl of porridge.

The room we ate in was opened to the yard and was almost as large and airy as the sitting room in my mother's home. Several baskets for storing clothing sat in one corner. Bright blue mats lay on the red clay floor. The room had a delicious fragrance of roses from Ajoa's perfume and from the fragrant wood that she had put into the fire, just as my mother did, in order to perfume the air.

Respectfully, I waited for her to speak.

"Did you sleep well?" she asked.

"No, Mistress. I could not stop thinking about my father and my brother." I searched for the right words to say to her. "Mistress, excuse me, but will your husband begin our journey today?"

"Oh, dear, he will not be able to take you back until the next full moon when he is finished with the harvest. This is a busy time, and he cannot leave now."

My heart sank. "But, Mistress, I must go back immediately. My father and brother are dead and the other family members don't even know. They have to have the ceremony for the dead."

"Kofi, it can't be helped. Be patient. He will take you back. My husband wants to return you safely himself, but he can't leave for a three-day journey now."

Although I trusted her and Atta, I was dejected and longed for my own family.

She took a sip of tea. "Kofi, when you're finished eating, I'll take you to Amu's compound. He's my husband's head drummer. You can pass the time with him and let him hear your song."

I was miserable as we left her house and the family compound. The village was awake and busy, and all that I saw reminded me of my own home. People were leaving their compounds to

40

walk to their farms. I caught a glimpse of a potter in his yard shaping his clay. The village goldsmith was immediately recognizable in his large golden bangles and anklets, as he left his compound followed by a servant.

As we entered the drummer's compound, a group of girls and women carrying bundles of cloth and pottery on their heads passed us. I knew that they were probably going to sell their wares, which meant that a market was nearby.

I spent the day at the drummer's compound, watching him make a talking drum. My mind, though, was only on the terrible things that had happened. I sat and waited for the sun to set, so that I would know what direction my home was in. If Atta changed his mind about helping me, I would find my own way home and get help for Kwesi. I was a great man's son and if I had to leave and find my way by myself, my father's spirit would protect me. I didn't need Atta or anyone else. My mood lifted, and I put my flute to my lips and played a happy song.

When I left the drummer's compound to return to Atta's, the long shadows cast by the setting sun were spreading in the direction of the cedar grove. I then knew the way to my own village.

Ajoa asked me to play my flute after we ate. The whole compound was gathered in Atta's section of the courtyard. Some of the children and the elder members of the family were in Atta's sitting room, which opened to the courtyard. Atta and Ajoa sat on couches built into the wall and covered with leopard skins and other animal hides. Blue, red, and dark orange mats decorated the earthen floor.

I stood at the entrance so that those inside and outside could hear me. As I played, the stars came out, the children laughed and danced, and the women's eyes shone like gold. I played my own song, no tune I'd ever heard or that Oppong had taught me. I played the joy in my heart, knowing that I would soon be with my family. "I wish you could stay and be my musician," Atta said. He then looked at his sour-faced son. "While you're here, Kofi, I want you to teach Kwaku how to play like you. He only knows one or two songs."

And it probably rains every time he plays them, I said to myself.

"That's a wonderful idea," Ajoa smiled.

I didn't look at Kwaku's face, because I was sure he'd made it into a surly frown.

"Does that mean I don't have to work in the fields?" he asked his father.

"Of course you have to work! Kofi can teach you in the evening when you're done."

"Why doesn't he have to work?" he said, looking angrily in my direction.

"He is not my son, servant, or slave. He is a guest in our home."

Kwaku said no more, but I knew he was angry

and humiliated. One of his sisters giggled, and everyone begged me to play another song. Only Kwaku did not smile in my direction.

I was calmer and happier that night. As I lay on my mat and listened to the boys snoring, I made a decision. I could not wait for Atta to take me home. Kwesi needed help. My family needed to know that Father and Manu had been killed.

Ajoa said it was just a day-and-a-half-long journey from here. I would leave early in the morning before the roosters crowed and find my own way home.

VI
The Search

The cawing and chirping birds woke me up. The boys were all gone. I'd overslept. I quickly got up and peeped outside of the hut. No one was about yet. Kwaku and his brothers were probably in their mother's home having breakfast. I could still leave without being seen. I felt my hips, making sure that the purse was still there. Then I checked for my flute, which I kept beside me on my pallet. I didn't see it, so I felt under the pallet. It wasn't there. I searched around the floor. The flute was gone!

I lifted my pallet off the floor, throwing it, like a madman, in a corner. I looked for it under Kwaku's and the other boys' pallets. I searched through baskets where they kept their garments — not caring that I threw sandals and robes all over the room.

I knew it was there. Kwaku was hiding it — trying to upset me. I went through their belongings again — no flute. I flew out of the hut and began to claw at the ground in front. Maybe he buried it to trick me.

Atta's daughter passed me on her way to take her father his breakfast. She rested a bowl filled with porridge on the ground and squatted beside me. "What are you doing?"

"My flute," I cried. "My flute is gone, and I know one of your brothers, probably Kwaku, took it."

"I know where your flute is," she whispered.

I grabbed her thin shoulders, nearly knocking her down. "Where? Tell me."

"You won't say that I told you?"

"No. Please," I wailed desperately.

"Kwaku ran off to the market to sell it to Sharif, one of the traders."

Without another thought or word, I raced out of the compound. Maybe I could catch him before he reached the market. I ran past the drummer's compound and out to the road where I'd seen the women going to market the day before. Already the procession of market women, some with their children, walked down the road balancing baskets and bundles on their heads, like queens wearing heavy crowns.

I dashed along the side of the road, following the lines of women and a few men who were heading to the market. When I reached the big and busy marketplace, I was reminded of the festival at Kumasi. The market was just coming to life. Some of the women spread baskets of yams, beans, corn, potatoes, and other foods on the ground before them. Others displayed bundles of cloth woven in the colors of the earth and the sky.

Where would I find this trader, Sharif, among the market sellers and rows of stalls? I ran from stall to stall and seller to seller asking for a trader named Sharif. "I haven't seen him yet today," or "I'm not sure where he is," were the only answers I got.

I was near tears as I realized that I might never see my flute again. I was about to give up my search when I saw a large stall bursting with drums, Ashanti stools, the wide trousers and small caps from the Moorish country, copper and silver bangles, and bundles of cloth.

A girl, about my age, with eyes like two black moons, neatly folded finely woven white cloth on a mat that lay on the ground outside of the stall. She was dressed in the style of the Arabs. Her head and face were covered with a dark red shawl, showing only her beautiful black eyes.

"Do you know a seller named Sharif?" I asked her.

"Sharif is the trader here," she said in perfect Ashanti.

"Has a boy been here to sell him a flute?" I asked looking anxiously at all of the wares in front

46

of the stall. She began to arrange copper bangles next to the cloth.

"No one has been here."

"Where is Sharif?"

"I don't know, and why do you ask so many questions?"

"I want my flute!" I shouted angrily.

"I don't know anything about your flute, and don't you shout at me."

She walked around to the back of the stall, leaving me standing there with my arms folded. This Sharif would come to his stall at some time. I'd wait for him. The girl returned, carrying an armload of cloth, woven in blue and yellow, reminding me of the beautiful robe my father had given me.

"When will Sharif be back?" I asked.

Before she could answer, a voice said, "I am back. Who are you?"

I turned around to face a thin, wiry old man with two small eyes. "I'm looking for my flute. A boy named Kwaku took it from me, and I was told that he sold it to you."

"Me? Am I the only trader in this market?"

His eyes bore into mine, making me feel as if I were guilty of something. I turned away from him and glanced at the girl who was still arranging Sharif's goods. He reached inside a sack that he was carrying. "Is this your flute?"

"That's it," I shouted, reaching for the flute.

He pushed my arm away. The girl busied herself arranging bangles as if she were paying no attention to us.

"That's my flute. My father gave it to me." My story rolled out of my mouth as quickly as the tears rolled down my cheeks.

"You can buy the flute from me," Sharif said.

"But it's mine. Kwaku stole it from me."

"It doesn't matter. I paid well for it. You could be a clever liar trying to cheat an old man."

I sighed. "But, sir, it's mine. Everything I told you is true." I reached down into my loincloth and removed the goldweight. "This is all that I have."

He took it and examined it carefully. "It's not worth much. Not as valuable as the flute. It's only a goldweight." He handed it back to me.

"It is valuable among my people," I said. "It means, do not regret that which has already passed."

The trader smiled slightly. "That's a wise saying. And that's why I will not trade it for the flute, because I would surely regret it. You can work for me and I'll tell you when you've earned enough to pay for it."

I shook my head. "But it's mine. Why do I have to buy what's mine?"

"Can you prove it's yours?"

"I'll play it for you."

He squatted down in front of his wares and

picked up the flute. "Silly child. That's no proof. Any good musician can get a sound out of this flute."

"Not like the sound I get," I fired back. "Don't you know Kwaku, the boy who sold it to you?"

"No."

"He knows you. He told his sister that he was going to sell the flute to you."

"Everyone knows me. I'm the biggest trader in this market." He studied the flute carefully. "It's well crafted. I could get a good price for it. But I won't sell it to anyone. I'll only sell it to you for what I paid for it."

I sat down before him as if I, too, were a man. I studied him carefully and saw the gold coins in his eyes.

"Sir," I said, "if you give me back my flute and also return me to my family, they will give you gold. My story is true. My father was a great chief, and we have much gold."

Sharif stared through me as if he could read my soul.

"I am a busy man and have no time to deliver little Ashanti princes back to their families." He called the girl. "Ama, bring me some tea," he ordered. "So, you work for me and you'll get your flute back."

Maybe I should go back and tell Atta what Kwaku had done, I thought. But, if I left, Sharif would surely sell the flute.

49

"I'll work for you," I said, holding my head down so that he could not see the anger in my eyes.

Ama brought Sharif his tea. She glanced at me sympathetically while Sharif took his cup, stood up, and led me to the back of his stall. He put the flute in a bundle so that no buyer would see it. He then pointed to a pile of brass bowls and handed me a cloth and a bowl filled with oil. "Clean these."

I sat down and began to slowly rub a bowl. Out of the corner of my eye I saw Sharif tie the bundle securely, making many knots, and throw it over his thin shoulders. "Don't worry," he said, "I won't sell it." Yet my heart sank as he left with my treasure. I walked to the front of the stall where the girl was showing several customers Sharif's cloth and squatted down in front of the stall like a common servant or slave. I continued to rub the bowl, and the dirt and dark scratches gradually began to disappear. My father, who watched over me, would continue to protect me, and I'd get my flute back from Sharif and would soon, along with my brother, return to my father's house.

Loud laughter from the market women a few stalls away eased my troubled spirits. The light and happy sound of their voices reminded me of my mother and my sister, Afua. I imagined how they would both laugh and sing when Kwesi and I walked through the gates of our compound.

I spotted a tall, familiar figure resplendent in a blue robe with gold bangles covering his arm. A woman carrying a large basket filled with yams and other vegetables stood in front of me and I couldn't see him. I stood up to get a better look, and I hardly believed my eyes. There was Oppong with his legs spread slightly apart and his hands on his hips, smiling and talking to two women. I quickly stepped behind the stall so that he wouldn't see me and continued to watch him as my heart raced in fear and anger — how did he dare be so joyous after what he'd done?

VII
Escape

The girl left her customers and followed me to the back of the stall.

"What's wrong with you?" she asked.

I opened my mouth to speak, but I could only tremble. Her black-moon eyes were like the softest silk. "Calm yourself. Let me finish with the customers, and then you can tell me what happened."

Seeing Oppong brought back all my pain and horror. I sat in a corner of the stall and buried my face in my upraised knees. The girl quickly returned.

"What frightened you?" she asked.

"I saw Oppong," I said. "The man who had my father murdered." I described to her what he looked like and what he was wearing.

"I know the one in the blue robe. His name is Jamal, not Oppong."

"It's Oppong," I insisted.

"No, it's Jamal," she said. "He's a rich trader from the north. Everyone knows him. He just got here two days ago, and his gold flows like a river from his hands."

"I've known him all of my life," I retorted. "His name is Oppong. I don't care what he calls himself now. He took gold for killing my father. That's how he became rich."

I was beginning to understand where Oppong had disappeared to the day before we had arrived at Kumasi. He was making his plans and posing as a trader.

"Does Sharif know him?" I asked, fearful for my life.

"They've talked, but they're not friends."

"Does he come here to visit Sharif?"

"No. He only passed here once, but he talked to Sharif about forming a caravan of slaves to sell on the coast."

"I have to get away from here before he sees me, but I must get my flute back."

"Surely your life is worth more than your flute," Ama said.

"The flute was a present from my dear father," I said. "I must have it."

"Then you must stay hidden behind the stall and finish this work for Sharif. He will return your flute as he promised." I calmed down a bit.

The morning dragged on as I polished and rubbed bowls and brass lanterns behind the stall and listened to Ama wait on the customers. I jumped nervously each time I thought I heard footsteps approaching. When I thought that I couldn't polish another bowl, the girl came behind the stall and closed it for the midday meal.

"Sharif won't come back for a long while," she assured me. "He's at his other stalls in the Miminda market." She sat before me and handed me a bowl of water to wash my hands. She did the same.

"Don't worry about this Jamal or Oppong," she continued. "I will keep you safely hidden."

I watched her make mallaget, a dish of fish boiled with a handful of corn and dough and palm oil and wondered about this girl who dressed like a Muslim but spoke perfect Ashanti. "Why are you helping me?" I asked as she handed me the food.

She took her veil off. I knew that once Muslim girls wore veils, they never removed them in front of strangers. Her face was a beautiful as I'd imagined. Her lips were full and her nose spread like a slightly rising hill below her high cheekbones. I guessed that we were the same age.

"I don't belong to Sharif. I am like you and was stolen from my village. My name is Ama and I am Ashanti, too."

She took a bite of food. "I am not from a royal family like yours. My people are farmers, and our village was in a remote part of the kingdom. We lived in peace with our neighbors." Her eyes took on a faraway look as she told her story. "Many of the villages around us were raided by slave catchers. During the day, when the adults were off at their farms, we children had the job of climbing up the trees so that we could see anyone aproaching the village. We were to make certain bird calls as a signal to the adults that strangers were coming.

"The old people helped, too, and lined the path to our village with poison darts. We children loved this — it was better than fetching water and firewood. We sang and played up in the trees, and no one ever came to bother us.

"Then one day we saw them. A band of men way in the distance coming out of the hills. We raised our bird cries, and our mothers and fathers came from the opposite direction with their cutlasses in their hands to meet the strangers. But the cutlasses that they used to chop stalks in the fields were no match for the men's firesticks.

"Several of the men were poisoned by the darts, but that didn't help. I tried to run to my mother and father and was captured along with my brother. I heard only screams and cries. The men from my village were beaten and bound. Those who fought too hard were killed.

"My mother was chained to the other women. We children went with one group of men and the adults with another. The village was burned down. I don't know what happened to the old grandmothers and grandfathers. We saw five sunrises and sunsets before we came to a slave market. We were tired and sickly and could barely walk on our bleeding feet.

"I saw white men at this market. One of the whites bought all of the children from my village, including my brother. Sharif bought me. I was very sick, and he purchased me for a few cowrie shells. He only wanted a slave girl or boy to help him in the market.

"I have been with Sharif and his family for one season now. I dream of my family, but I know I'll never see them again."

She began to weep, and I held back my own tears as I rubbed her back, the way my mother used to rub mine when I was upset. "I thought you were a Muslim girl," I said.

"That's what Sharif wants to make me. He says I must follow his religion, and then I will be free. But I always tell myself that I am already free." She wiped her eyes. "I follow what he says, and he thinks I believe in his religion, but in my heart I am Ashanti and believe in the religion of my ancestors. Sharif wants to marry me to one of his sons when I am of age."

"You don't want to marry his son?"

"No. But what choice do I have. All my people are gone. I have no family of my own. My whole clan was destroyed with my village. Some people tell me that I am lucky I was not taken by the white man and put on his water house. I heard that those people are cooked and eaten and never seen again."

"Are they that wicked?" I touched her arm. "Ama, when I get my flute, I am leaving. You can come with me. My family will welcome you to our village."

"Why would they go to so much bother for me?"

"You were kind to me. And you are Ashanti. They will treat you like a daughter, I know it." I took a last bite of the food. "Maybe some of the people returned to your village once the raiders left," I said.

Her face brightened. "Yes, and perhaps my mother and father got away from the kidnappers. Do you think they are in the village?"

"They could be. Perhaps they have returned and are looking for you."

She smiled sweetly. "You are friendlier than I first supposed. What's your name?"

"Kofi."

She stood up. "You better get to work, Kofi, so that Sharif will return your flute."

"Ama, will you leave with me? My family will help you."

She sighed deeply and covered her face once again with her veil. "But suppose the village is empty. I couldn't bear to see it. I have to think about leaving with you," she said, her voice filled with doubt.

57

"I must leave soon. I have to tell my family that Oppong is here, and if I stay too long, he is bound to see me."

"I must open the stall. Stay back here and keep out of sight."

As she left, I nervously peeked from behind the stall, but I didn't see Oppong. Ama was busy selling while I rubbed and polished until every bowl, bangle, and lantern was shining.

When it was time to leave, we put Sharif's goods behind his stall and waited for him. He arrived with several young servant boys. They carried his bundles, but Sharif himself bore the sack that held my flute.

"Sir," I bowed slightly, "I've finished polishing."

"Wonderful, but you haven't earned that flute yet. I have more work for you tomorrow."

I fought my rage. Was this old Arab trying to make me work for him forever? We walked silently to his village, which sat in the direction of the setting sun, several miles from Atta's village. He had a large compound, and once we entered I didn't see Ama. She walked through the entranceway of a long house closed in on all sides and disappeared inside the home with the other women and girls of the family.

I ate a lonely and miserable meal sitting outside of the hut where we were to sleep. I ignored the laughter and talk of Sharif's servant boys. Speaking Fanti, they tried to make friends with me, but I made believe that I didn't understand their language. I didn't want to talk to anyone except Ama. And I wanted my flute. I would get it back, even if I had to take it out of Sharif's bundle myself.

That night when we were inside the hut, I listened to the boys' contented snores as I planned how I was going to find my flute and get away from Sharif.

I drifted off to sleep but was startled awake by someone shaking me gently. "Kofi, Kofi. It's me, Ama. Wake up."

I jumped up. "What's wrong?"

"Shush." She put her finger to her lips and pulled my arm. One of the boys moaned in his sleep, while I almost stumbled over another. Out of habit I checked for the goldweight around my hips. We stepped out into the dark and crouched down by the hut. She reached inside the basket that she'd left at the entrance. "Here's your flute. May Nyame will forgive me taking what's not mine, but it is not Sharif's either. It is yours."

"Ama, you are the most wonderful person in the world," I said. "How did you . . ."

Ama put her finger over my lips again. "I'll tell you later," she whispered. "But we must leave now. I have decided to go with you, Kofi." She pointed past the compound walls to a thin thread of light. "We have to go that way, where the sun rises."

My heart leaped inside of my chest. I was going home.

"We must leave now before everyone is up."

She put her basket on top of her head, and we crouched in the shadow of the trees as we headed toward the compound gate. We left the compound in the dark of dawn and walked hurriedly through the village. Some people were already up, as we could smell the smoke from the various compounds where the women were beginning to prepare the morning meal. We walked close to the walls so that no one would see us. I was glad, though, that it was not completely dark, but that strange time between night and day. We did not stop to talk, for we wanted to be as far away from the village as possible before Sharif found out we were missing. When we reached a grove of cedar trees we finally stopped to rest and eat after walking for many hours. The mallaget Ama had brought in her basket tasted delicious. After we'd eaten our fill, we talked. "How did you get the flute?" I asked her.

Happily, she removed her veil and put it into her basket. Her whole face seemed to smile as her ebony eyes sparkled. "Sharif had visitors, and he wasn't in his quarters. I went into his room, opened the bundle, and removed your flute."

"Weren't you afraid of being caught?"

"Yes," she said, lowering her eyes, "but I wanted to help you because you're so kind to me."

She leaned against a tree trunk. "But had he caught me, I would have said that I was counting the goods as I usually do to remind him of what we have or need."

"Ama," I took her small soft hands in mine, "you're the bravest girl in the kingdom, and when we reach my village my family will honor you like a queen."

Smiling, she stood up. "I think we should move along, Kofi, so that by nightfall we will find a safe place to sleep."

As we began to walk again, Ama made sure the food that we were saving to eat later was covered with cloth and that her veil was tucked safely inside the basket. Contentedly we walked in the sweet fresh air of a new morning, and we both jumped with a start when something moved from behind the bushes nearby. A sharp breeze parting the leaves revealed the hind parts of a hare under a bush. We laughed with relief.

"Don't worry, Ama, we're not deep in the forest," I said. "See how the ground is smooth where we're walking and not overgrown with bush? That means that people travel this route and villages are nearby."

"How do you know that?" she asked, picking up her pace.

"That devil Oppong taught me about the forest. If we stay on this path, we'll come to a village by nightfall."

We walked until the sun began to set. Though I kept a brave face for Ama, I was nervous at the thought of spending the night in the forest. "We'll build a fire to keep the animals away if there are any about."

Just before dark, we found a spot where the tops of a group of small trees intertwined forming a canopy of leaves. "This seems like a good place to stay for the night," I said. Resting my flute on the ground, I began to gather twigs to build a fire.

Ama looked around, sniffing. "I smell smoke from cooking fires."

"It's coming from over there," I said, pointing to a thicket of vines. "There's a village close by."

"Let's go there and ask for help," she suggested.

"No. That is what Sharif would expect us to do. He'd be sure to find us. We're safe here for the night."

We made a fire and built an enclosure out of twigs and leaves under the small grove of trees. Ama spread her veil on the ground as a covering for us to sit on while we ate some more of the mallaget. We listened to a rising chorus of crickets and other night insects. "Don't be afraid, Ama, the ancestors will protect us."

Thinking that I heard a hyena in the distance, I picked up my flute and played a song that my sister used to sing. Ama knew it, too, and sang along. The music silenced the night creatures that I imagined I heard and removed our fear. When our eyes grew heavy with sleep, we lay huddled together in our makeshift enclosure, wrapped up in Ama's veil.

My pounding heart was louder than the night sounds, and if Ama had not been with me I think that I would have died of fright. "Are you afraid, Ama?" I asked her.

"Yes, Kofi. Are you?"

"No," I said softly. "I'm not afraid."

Ama stroked my head the way my mother would have. "The ancestors are watching over us," she whispered, "and we'll watch over each other."

Her words soothed me, and I fell fast asleep.

The sun, like a warm hand, touched our faces the next morning. Ama still slept, breathing softly next to me. The sharp air and clear morning light along with the sounds of birds chirping and faint voices from the nearby village made me feel like a brave Ashanti. I had survived a night in the forest, I thought proudly.

I went behind a tree to relieve myself. When I returned to the shelter, Ama was sitting up and rubbing her eyes. "Oh, Kofi, when I woke up I thought that I was still at Sharif's." She reached inside her basket and took out two juicy, red pomegranates. "Here's our morning meal." She rummaged through the basket. "We have a little mallaget left for tonight."

"That's all we'll need," I said confidently. "By the next sunrise, we will have reached my village — or one of our neighboring villages." I took another bite of the fruit. "We'll be safe from Sharif in any Ashanti village."

We both ate another piece of fruit and watched the birds and a pair of black-and-white monkeys flit across the trees. The world was so different during the day.

"I wonder whether Sharif is looking for us," I said.

Ama took the last bite out of her fruit. "Maybe he searched for a while, but I think by now he's given up," she said. "He's probably already replaced me with another slave to work in the market."

I picked up my flute. "He's angry about this flute, I know."

"Well, it wasn't his flute."

I stood up. "We'd better leave now."

Ama folded her veil and put it in her basket.

Walking quickly along a well-traveled path, we stopped only once to pick wild berries. "We will feast like a king and queen on cold, dried mallaget and berries," Ama announced.

We walked for many hours. And when the sun was at its strongest, we stopped to rest under a tree and eat the berries we'd picked in the morning. I saw a wonderful sight. "Oh, Ama," I cried, "look."

"What is it?"

I pointed to a large akata tree a few feet away from us. "Look at the bowls under that tree. They're turned upside down, and each one has a stone on top of it."

She grabbed my arm. "We are near an Ashanti village, Kofi." Ama stood up slowly and walked over to the tree. Her smile was as bright as the sun. "The upside-down bowls are an Ashanti custom. People come here to pray for their health and crops and leave an offering under the akata tree."

We practically danced in each other's arms. "Let's find the village. We can sleep there and not spend another night in the forest," I said excitedly. Our feet and hearts were light as we walked along the path. I played my flute, making up a happy tune, and Ama created words to go with my song. "We are returning to our people who will help us find our home," she sang.

We'd only been walking a short while when she stopped singing. "I hear voices," she said. "Like the sounds of children playing."

"Where?" I asked, my heart swelling with excitement.

"Straight ahead, past those cedar trees. Where the Ashanti village is."

As we raced toward the grove of trees, we heard a monkey screech and leaves rustling behind us. I turned around speechless and terrified, as my legs turned suddenly to stone. For I found myself staring straight into Sharif's angry eyes.

VIII
The Coast

Sharif was accompanied by two black men dressed in the uniform of the whites — tight trousers and long, black boots. I'd learned that black men dressed in this manner were usually involved with the white slave traders, and these men were no exception.

Sharif grabbed Ama and pointed at me. I started to run, but one of the men snatched my arm, making me drop my flute.

"Take him and give me what we agreed," Sharif said. The man handed him a purse, and Sharif counted the coins. My blood ran cold as I felt echoes of my recent experience with Oppong.

Sharif turned to a shaking and crying Ama, as Ama struggled to replace the veil over her face.

"I know you only ran away because of the little Ashanti devil. Tell me, are you a follower of the true religion? If not, then go with him and be a slave to the foreigners. Would you rather be a slave than a daughter in my household?"

He slapped her and I lunged toward him, but

one of the men knocked me down. I could not protect her.

"You're in my household." He grabbed her arm. "Our women do not run away."

She cried bitterly, and I felt all of her pain. We had become like brother and sister, and I was to blame for her trouble. With my free hand I pulled my purse containing the goldweight from around my waist and handed it to her.

"Don't look back. Go with him," I said. I was defeated, for each time I tried to return to my home I fell into deeper trouble.

"She doesn't need advice from you," Sharif hurled back at me. She picked up the goldweight and gazed at me sadly. Then she turned to Sharif. "I am a believer," she muttered, staring at the ground. She clutched the goldweight, and Sharif picked up my flute and handed it to me. "Here. You've paid for this with your very own self. Now you belong to these men."

With great heaviness in my heart, I walked for many hours between the two men — where to, I did not know. We did not stop to rest. The men spoke a language foreign to me. At sunset we arrived at a small compound, and I was led to a hut where we rested for the night. I was given soup and could hear people talking outside.

"I have to wash before I eat," I said to the men but they couldn't understand me. One of them lifted the bowl to my mouth, but I refused to eat even though I was starving. He left me alone. I cradled my flute in my arms as if it were a baby. Regrets poured down on me like rain. I should not have followed Father to the forest. I should have had more patience and remained at Atta's home. I should not have asked Ama to run away with me.

When we started out the following day, I saw the sun rising behind the hills and thought of my home. It was farther away than ever, now, and there was no way of escaping from my new kidnappers.

We walked for many hours again that day. We did stop at a stream where I was able to wash myself. I ate some dried fish the men offered me. The country we were in looked different from what I was accustomed to. The hills were high and green. It was beautiful country, and had I not been taken away from everyone and everything that I loved I would have been happy to be there.

We slept in the open that night. The men built a fire and made a shelter from branches and leaves.

The third morning, as we walked away from the rising sun, I spotted a tremendous caravan of hundreds of people and cattle making its way down the side of a hill. When we drew closer, I saw men carrying great bundles of animal hides, tusks of ivory, and chests, which I imagined were filled with gold. But as they were passing, I was shocked to catch the frightening sight behind the animals — about one hundred boys and girls chained to one another by the waist. None of them looked older than fifteen seasons.

Men with guns walked near them, and I knew where I was headed. This was a caravan taking gold, ivory, and slaves to the coast. My two captors led me to a man dressed in a flowing white robe, and carried by servants on a hammock. A white man was also carried alongside him. I wanted to tell them that I was the son of a great chief and should not be made a slave, but fear and all that had happened to me rendered me speechless. It seemed that every time I was close to becoming free and happy, I became a captive once again. I had lost my home, my family, and even myself. I was a slave, dressed in a filthy loincloth. I could hardly even remember what my beautiful robe looked like.

With my flute tucked safely inside my loincloth, I was chained to another boy. He said something to me, but I could not understand his language. We walked for the rest of the day. The boy stumbled often, and I thought he might be sick. After two more sunrises and sunsets, the boy died and was left to the jackals and buzzards.

Finally, after traveling for one more day, we reached the coast. The salty air smelled strange to me. For this was the first time in my life I'd been near the ocean. I'd only seen fresh-water streams and small ponds in my forest kingdom.

We were led into a building made of cane stalks covered with a thatched roof. The smell of unclean human bodies took my breath away, and I lay on the clay floor chained to another boy. I held my flute and cried myself to sleep. The next morning I was offered some gruel to eat, which I refused even though I was weak and hungry.

The place was filled with men and women and even babies still clinging to their mothers. When we were led out of the slave pen, the bright light hurt my eyes as much as the sights I saw.

The buildings that stood in the hot, humid air were all made from cane stalks like the one we had been imprisoned in. What shocked me the most was the great numbers of white men in their strange-looking tight trousers and wide straw headdresses. I saw black men who wore the clothing of the whites and carried firesticks.

We were led away from the rows and rows of buildings toward the water. Hundreds of other people — men and women with great iron shackles around their necks and ankles were also being taken to the beach. Our group, though, was made up only of children.

The same white man who was in the caravan led us toward the beach. When we got there, I saw for the first time in my life a fort with a cannon at the top facing the water. I also saw the white men's water houses rising and falling on the waves. Tears streamed down my face as I felt for the flute under my loincloth and turned around to gaze at the sun. The boy behind me cried, too.

When we reached the beach, men, women, and even a few young children filed into the fort. The white men examined the people in chains the same way that I've seen men examine a goat or a cow before purchasing it — squeezing a man's arms, his legs, then peering inside his mouth and ears — pulling his eyes open. One man shouted something at his examiner in a strange language, but the white man slapped him sharply and yelled back. Even though the prisoner was strong and healthy, there was nothing that he could do because his hands and feet were bound.

One moment became more horrifying than the next as I saw another white man pick up a glowing hot iron and press it between the prisoner's shoulder blades. He shrieked in pain as one of the blacks dressed in white man's dress rubbed palm oil on the mark the iron had made.

The white man continued up and down the lines of men and women branding them with the same iron. Some of the women cried when they were made to take off their cloths so that they too could be examined. I turned away, feeling as much shame as the women did.

We were quickly led away, and instead of going to one of the canoes that were ferrying prisoners to the water houses, we were taken past the fort to a lagoon. There, boys, separated from girls, were unshackled and allowed to bathe. I carefully placed my cloth on top of my flute and splashed the water over me. The boy who had been chained to me in the slave pen spoke Fanti, which I could understand because it was similar to Ashanti. "We're only going to the white man's water house to work a while. Then we'll be returned to our families," he informed me.

I felt hopeful. When we finished bathing, we were given palm oil to rub our bodies with, and then we were made to sit in a grove of palm trees and were given a delicious meal of fish soup. For the first time I tasted coconut meat, which I loved. We ate as much food as we wanted. I ate well because I had washed.

After we were cleaned, well fed, and rested, the same white man who'd been with the caravan came over to us and smiled as he talked to the guards.

My heart sank as we were once again chained together and led to the shore and the waiting canoes. It was our turn to be examined like animals. The girls cried and tried to cover their nakedness. I closed my eyes so that I wouldn't have to look into the terrifying blue eyes of the man who examined me.

We were unchained and pushed into the waiting canoes. Several boys tried to stand up and jump, but were knocked down by the oarsman. Canoes, filled with men and women in chains making their way to the waiting ships, covered the water. Why would these men need so many people to work in their water houses? Maybe they were going to eat some of us as Ama had said. I trembled, fearing that I would never see my beloved home or family again.

I tried to stand up in the rocking canoe. I would return to my ancestors rather than go with these foreigners. Someone pushed me back down. But in that moment that I'd stood, I saw a familiar face in one of the canoes near us — Oppong with his blue robe soiled and in shreds and a big iron clamp around his neck.

I shot up again. "Oppong!" I yelled. He turned his head and looked at me for a short moment, until one of the men rowing the boat pushed me down again. Oppong's fortunes had changed as quickly as mine. Someone must have found out that he was not a rich trader from the north, but a criminal, and had him sold. Kwesi said that Oppong would certainly be punished for his deeds. Perhaps it was Ama who revealed his lies.

My surprise at seeing Oppong, however, was nothing compared to the terror that overcame me as we neared the waiting ship.

IX
The Slaver

I closed my eyes and ran my fingers over the circles and lines carved into my flute. I didn't want to see what stood before me or even believe that I was on the dreaded white man's water house.

When I opened my eyes, I saw only a black hole as the same white man from the caravan led me and about 100 other children down to the bottom of the ship. He shouted at the crewmen as he supervised, squeezing all of us into tiny berths. Even I could not stand up straight in that small space, nor could the tallest boys and girls lie straight. We lay in one another's laps.

As the crewman passed by my berth, he saw my flute and reached for it, and I bit his hand. He grabbed me by my neck and flung me to the floor. My head hit the floor with such force, I fainted into unconsciousness.

When I regained consciousness, I found myself on the deck of the ship. I thought that I had entered the kingdom of the dead — and that it was all water.

A pungent bitterness filled my nostrils and my mouth as one of the men tried to force a cup of a horrible-smelling liquid between my lips. I clenched my teeth, refusing to swallow it. A young man, who I thought was Ashanti, took the cup from him and offered me the liquid. I accepted it from the young man and drank. It burned terribly as it went down, and the men laughed as I spat and sputtered and coughed. But the boy seemed as if he were trying to tell me something. I spoke to him in my language, thinking that he would understand. He looked at me sympathetically but understood nothing I said.

He spoke to me again, and I wondered why he used the pale man's language and did not speak in a tongue that I knew. He then handed me a bowl of terrible-smelling gruel, saying the Fanti word for eat, but it was pronounced in such an unusual manner that I did not understand him at first. I answered him in Fanti, telling him that I could not eat without first washing my hands. He still did not understand. He kept putting the food in front of me while pointing to a frightening object near me that was shaped like a long drum with rope wound around it. His eyes darted from me to the drumlike object. I continued to refuse to eat and rubbed my hands together indicating that I had to wash them. He shook his head.

One of the crewmen pushed him aside and

tried to pull open my clamped mouth. Next, the chief of the ship, his face as wide and red as a mango, stomped over to us. The crewmen scampered like mice. The sounds from his mouth were more horrible than the others. On his orders, one of the men pulled me over to the object, tied me to it, and beat me with a stinging whip. I screamed and cried in pain. Never in my life had I been treated in such a savage manner. I understood then that the boy was telling me that if I didn't eat I'd be beaten. But I was determined not to eat the foul-smelling gruel and if their plan was to cook and eat me, then I'd make sure that I wasn't a fat, juicy calf.

I do not know how long I lay there bloodied and weak. The same mango-faced chief returned and ordered one of his men to force open my mouth. He tried to push the food in. I threw it up and was beaten again. I willed myself to die and seemed to pass to and fro between the world of the living and the spirit world. I saw my father and dreamed that Kwesi and I were returning to our village. I heard Ama crying, but when I awoke I found myself covered with a filthy blanket in a corner of the ship. I shivered with cold one minute and burned with fever the next.

Then I beheld a sight. The children who were in the bottom of the ship climbed up out of the ship's hold. They held small tin bowls, and the big, fat cook gave each a portion of the horrible gruel. The giant white wings of the water house flapped in the wind, and we were moving. Suddenly screams pierced the salt air as a girl jumped overboard. Her hands reached to the sky and then vanished under a wave.

Two other girls and a boy tried to follow her but the sailors pulled them away from the railing before they could jump.

I tried to get up so that I could join them, as that was the only way out of this horror, but in my weakened state, my head spun and I fell back down on the dirty blanket. I recited in my head the Ashanti prayer for the girl's spirit.

Scuffling and confusion erupted as the crewmen, yelling and shouting, tried to push everyone back down into the hold, while more and more of the children reached the rails and dove overboard. When the remaining captives were returned to the hold, the captain strode the deck in a rage as the crew skulked away from him. I gazed around for the boy who had befriended me, but I didn't see him.

I was still in pain from the beating and envied the children who had escaped. They would return to their ancestors.

The sun was setting — soon this long horrible day would close. The only sound I heard was water lapping against the sides of the ship. By the time it was dark, I heard other sounds: the children in the hold of the ship; the voices of men;

and then, a familiar sound — my flute. Someone was playing a low, foreign-sounding melody on my flute. In all of my pain and confusion, I hadn't realized that I no longer had it. I knew the sound of my instrument though it played a stranger's song.

I propped myself up on one elbow and peered around the dark deck, following the sounds of the music and men. In the light of a lantern, I saw a group of the crewmen along with the boy who had helped me. A sailor played my flute. Another boy, with a head of thick, yellow hair and a thin, white face sat with them. He was about fourteen seasons and seemed a strange creature to me since I had never before seen a white boy — only white men. It was hard, then, for me to think of him as a real human — the colorless face and the yellow hair. I was repelled and fascinated at the same time.

The rhythm of the song quickened, and Yellow Hair jumped up and stomped his feet in time to the music coming out of my flute. The men clapped and sang as the boy danced. I was painfully reminded of our own singing and dancing at our annual festival.

I stood up on shaky legs and stumbled toward the group. "That is my flute," I said hoarsely, tears streaming down my face. At first no one even noticed me; then the black boy stood up and came toward me. "The flute is mine," I continued to cry out. The men stopped singing, and the one playing my flute removed it from his lips and held it like a club shaking it at me and laughing.

Yellow Hair stopped dancing, and the black boy led me back to my corner, speaking to me soothingly. Once again I picked up a few Fanti-sounding words. "Rest," he said. "Beat you." The man started playing again, but Yellow Hair no longer danced. He followed us, and I turned away from him, for he seemed not real to me.

I lay back on the blanket, continuing to sob. Both boys tried to console me. I couldn't look at the white child, with his yellow hair that resembled a headdress made from a horse's mane and his face that resembled a mask.

I didn't stop crying until the man stopped playing. The boys talked quietly to one another, and I drifted off to a restless, tortured sleep, dreaming that night that Ama and I had returned to my village.

The next morning I woke up when someone shook me hard. When I looked into Yellow Hair's thin face, I remembered where I was. Grinning, he handed me my flute. Anger rose in me like the swelling sea. I snatched it from him and cradled it in my arms. It was all that I had left of my former life, and no matter what happened I would not let anyone ever take it from me again.

X
Friends

I tried to keep track of the days and the position of the sun. But it was difficult because I was so sick that I could not tell how much time had passed while I slept.

The captain examined me and ordered the black boy to give me the same kind of bitter liquid I was given my first day here. I drank, for I was too weak to refuse, and I trusted the boy who looked as if he'd come from my village.

I saw a young man, shivering and curled almost into a ball, lying near me. Several children lay on the deck, their spirits waiting for death to free them.

The captain stared at me and shouted to the cook who stood before a boiling cauldron. The thought of the food made my stomach heave. I tried to sit up, but was too weak. The cook yelled, and the black boy appeared, handing me a tin bowl. "Eat, eat," he said in Fanti. "Otherwise, they beat you."

The captain stood over me with the long painful whip in his hands. I couldn't bear any more blows, so I put the food in my mouth. Fear and a great will helped me to keep the food down. The captain walked away while the boy watched me. I detected a faint smell, like dead flesh from the hold below, and felt the food traveling up from my stomach. I began to heave. The boy scurried away, quickly returning with a bucket and a clean, wet piece of cloth. I vomited the food I'd just forced down and washed my hands with the cloth.

He emptied the bucket and then returned with another bowl of gruel. I shook my head, no. He quickly pushed aside the food with a dirty hand, and I saw coconut meat and a piece of fish. I understood. I was to pretend that I was consuming the mush while secretly eating the coconut meat and fish he handed me. When no one was looking, he threw the gruel overboard and went boldly to the man who gave out the food to show him my empty tin plate. The man piled more gruel on the plate, and the boy gave it to me, winking and handing me at the same time coconut meat and fish. Again, he threw away the gruel when I finished eating my fish and coconut.

He came back to me and, pointing to himself, said in his broken Fanti, "My name is Joseph."

I must have mangled his name, for he laughed and said the word again. "Joseph."

"Joseph," I repeated. He smiled, nodding his head.

I pointed to myself. "Kofi," I said.

He repeated it in a strange sounding way, and it was my turn to laugh.

"Are they going to eat me?" I asked him in Ashanti.

He didn't understand. I pointed to myself and said in Fanti, "Eat, eat." He got up quickly and returned with more coconut meat. I shook my head and pointed again to myself and the crewmen.

Slowly, it dawned on him what I had been asking, and he threw his long head back and laughed. I didn't think my being eaten was funny. He then helped me to understand, using a poorly spoken mixture of Twi and Fanti and some other words that I could not make out at all, along with hand and body movements, that I would not be eaten.

I realized that he'd learned bits of the languages of the various captives that he'd met on the ships, but that the language he spoke most naturally was the white man's tongue.

"Joseph," the fat cook yelled as he stirred the cauldron. Joseph jumped and ran. I repeated his odd name over and over again. It was some comfort for me to know the name of at least one person in this place — and that someone knew mine — even if he could not pronounce it properly.

I saw Yellow Hair again, and he was straining and pulling at the ropes while the same man who'd taken my flute shouted at him and beat him across his head and ears. The savagery of these people amazed me. Joseph pulled open the hatch on the floor of the deck, and I lost my breath when the horrible odor that I'd noticed faintly before I ate seemed to enclose me like a foul-smelling blanket. My stomach was in my mouth again as I watched Joseph and Yellow Hair climb down to the hold of the ship.

The children who had been lying near me remained still. My cloth was ragged and filthy — how I longed to wash and have a clean body again.

That evening the same crewman who'd taken my flute stomped across the deck shouting. This was the time when they'd drink and play their music. Joseph and Yellow Hair sat with a group of men, and when the angry crewman wasn't looking, Yellow Hair and Joseph made the ugliest faces at him. The man must have just discovered that the flute was missing. It was hidden underneath my blanket, and I was determined that the crewman would not get it again.

I peeked into the dark corners near me, seeking a good place to hide my flute. I saw larger containers in one corner and thought of hiding it behind one of them. But I couldn't bear to let the flute out of my hands.

The man shouted at Yellow Hair, who stood up and let the sailor search him. He searched Joseph also. When he finished he grabbed both boys by the backs of their necks and knocked their heads together.

All of the men roared with laughter. The cook's stomach rose and fell like a fat wave. The two boys started to walk away, but one of the crewmen called them, making them provide a form of entertainment that I'd never seen before.

Joseph and Yellow Hair were made to fight one another while the men cheered one or the other boy. I was shocked by this inhuman activity. The boys barely tapped each other at first, but the men shouted and yelled and made threatening gestures toward them. One older man, with lines creasing his face like a fallow field, balled his fist at the boys and pointed at the same object that I'd been beaten on.

Yellow Hair slammed Joseph across his face and Joseph hit him so hard his nose bled. Both boys were the same height, but Yellow Hair was a little heavier than Joseph, who was tall and slender. The men were in a frenzy — yelling and pitching coins in a pile.

Both Joseph and Yellow Hair seemed as if they would cry, and I felt so sorry for them, for they were friends. I could watch no longer, but lay down and turned my back to the brutish game. I dreaded to think what I would do if I were forced to join in their sport.

The next day, Joseph's face was swollen, and Yellow Hair had a gash over his cheek. When Joseph brought my food, through our odd way of communicating with hand movements and Fanti words here and there I asked him Yellow Hair's name. "Timothy," Joseph said. His smile was painful as I tried to pronounce the name: "Timo . . . Timo . . ."

"Tim," Joseph said, "Tim."

While we were talking, the crewmen suddenly swarmed onto the deck. Several of them carried another crewman who had died, and I watched in horror as his body was wrapped in cloth and thrown overboard without a single prayer for his spirit. I quietly recited our prayer for the man's spirit. Even though he was not Ashanti, he was a living thing and his spirit had to be appeased.

My misery overwhelmed me, and often I considered jumping overboard as the girl had done, but the hope of seeing my family, and even Ama, again kept me in the world of the living. These people had great magic, I thought. And the magic was in those large wings that pounded against the wind. If I could learn the magic that moved this water house, then I could find my way home.

As Tim walked over to Joseph and me, I pointed to one of the magic things.

"Sails," Joseph said.

I repeated, "Sails." The way I said these strange words seemed to amuse him. Tim imitated my pronunciation. I pointed to another one of the mysterious objects — the thing that the men peered through all the time.

"Quadrant," Joseph said and I repeated it.

I pointed to the object I'd been tied to and beaten on when I first came on the ship.

"Windlass," Joseph said. I then pointed to the corner where the firesticks, cutlasses, and knives were stacked. I knew what these were and what they were used for. I turned away from them as they reminded me of my father and brother's brutal murder.

"Joseph! Tim!" one of the crewmen yelled. He ran over to us and jerked Joseph's arm vigorously and gave Tim a swift kick in the pants. They both scrambled away.

I looked again at the knives and cutlasses. Maybe if I had a weapon I could get away from these men. But where would I go. I no longer knew where the sun rose and set or where the land had gone to.

That evening when the men drank and sang in their corner of the deck, Tim sat with Joseph and me. Tim and Joseph talked to one another. I was glad for their company, even though I could not say much to them or understand what they said. I was curious about them. Were they slaves or freeborn? At first I thought that Tim was the son of one of the crewmen, but he was abused and knocked about as much as Joseph was. Often I would sit and wonder about them. Where were they born? Where were their families? Did they miss their homes the way I missed mine? How did they get here?

Each night Joseph and Tim sat with me teaching me more of their words. I listened to the sounds and was soon able to imitate them well. Tim no longer seemed strange to me. I was becoming accustomed to his yellow hair and pale green eyes that lit up when he mocked the crewmen behind their backs.

I was allowed to stay on deck since I remained in a weakened state. One evening, as Joseph, Tim, and I sat in a corner of the deck, I noticed that the moon was full. The last time I'd seen a full moon was the night that I had arrived at Atta's compound. Many days and nights had passed since I'd been away from home. Where was Kwesi, I wondered. By now my mother and the rest of the clan must know that something terrible had happened to Kwesi, Manu, Father, and me.

When I woke the next morning, the ship seemed as if it were barely moving. However, the sailors were dashing to and fro, pulling on the ropes and tying up the barrels and other containers. Instead of serving his nasty gruel, the cook was dragging his cauldron to the lower deck. The captain, his face as red as a berry, barked to the men as he rushed up and down the crowded deck. I didn't see Joseph or Tim. One of the crewmen shoved the boy who had been lying near me down into the hold of the ship. He was probably going to come for me next. I pretended that I was sleeping and held onto my flute, hidden beneath the blanket.

Someone shook me, and I opened my eyes and looked into Joseph's worried face. I had no idea what he was trying to tell me. He tried to pull me up, but I resisted. I couldn't understand why he was acting so strangely. He wrapped the blanket around me like a robe and pointed to the hold. "I don't want to go down there," I shouted in my language. He couldn't understand me, and I couldn't understand the words from his mouth, but his eyes seemed to beg. Why was he trying to force me to go in the stinking hold?

He pushed me and I jerked away from him, clutching the blanket around my shoulders and my flute underneath the blanket. Then with an exasperated look on his face he pointed to the sky. Great dark clouds had gathered like a flock of vultures. The sky god speaks a language that all men understand. A storm was approaching, but I still did not want to go down in the hold.

I backed away from Joseph's grasp and fell into the corner where the weapons were kept. I put

89

my hand on a cutlass, but when I saw the hurt look in Joseph's eyes, I dropped it.

"Please," I begged, "don't make me go down there. You are my friend."

He didn't understand my words, but he understood my wishes. He picked up a length of rope and wrapped it around his waist and quickly tied another piece of rope around my waist. He pulled me along and pushed me and himself to a thick pole and lashed us both to it.

It was dark as night as the clouds covered the sun and thunder roared over us. A mountain of water rose under the ship turning it on its side. I tried to yell, but my mouth filled with water as we were consumed by the sea. This is not a storm, I thought, for I had seen storms in my forest kingdom. This is the fury of the spirits raging because the men on the ship have never prayed for the spirits of the dead that they had thrown into the sea.

Barrels loosened from the rails and came crashing across the deck. Wood and sails flew around us as lightning danced across the deck. I heard in the thunder the angry voices of the gods. I prayed for my ancestors to come and save me, lest I be punished by the spirits for something that I did not do.

When the storm finally subsided, some of the sailors lay on the deck. Others sat dazed, rubbing their faces and arms. The captain held his head as he gazed around at the wood, sails, barrels, and debris strewn across the deck.

Joseph untied both of us, and I crawled into a corner. One of the crewmen opened the hatch to the hold and went down. He quickly returned and signaled for other crewmen to follow him. As each sailor came back up he carried a body. I prayed for the thirty children who had passed away from this world into the next.

Ten children had survived, including myself, Joseph, and Tim. Most of the sailors must have died, for I saw only a few of them after the storm. I huddled in a corner with the other children as the remaining crew spent the rest of the day repairing the sails and cleaning the ship.

A few days after the storm, I began to notice a smell of sickness and death covering the ship like a shroud. "It's the pox," Joseph told me. I saw no more children my age. The only ones left were five girls who had seen fourteen or fifteen seasons.

Each day, more corpses were thrown overboard. Those children who had been lying near me all died. The men who worked on the ship began to cover their noses and mouths with cloths. Many of them, too, were taken ill and were dying from the sickness aboard the ship.

Lethargy seemed to have overtaken everyone. The men did not drink and sing or make Timothy and Joseph fight. The fat cook boiled his gruel in his cauldron slowly, not screaming for Joseph as he usually did. The other men moved slowly about their tasks. The wind itself was lazy, just barely ruffling the sails. The captain was not bellowing like a bull, but remained in his quarters. The man whom I called the bringer of death, because each time he examined someone the body was sent over the side of the ship, looked frightened himself.

When the skies and water turned from blue to gray and the air became frigid, I entered a bitter and bleak new world.

XI
Bought and Sold

Boston, Massachusetts
November 1788

I pulled my blanket tightly around my shoulders and trembled so hard I thought that my teeth would fall out of my mouth. Never had I felt such cold nor seen such a gray sky. I was convinced that the evil spirits had won the battle at sea and we had been taken to their side.

When land could be seen in the distance, the crewmen pulled in the ragged sails, and the ship remained on the waters far away from shore. Joseph, Tim, and the remaining crew scrubbed the decks, hammered torn planks of wood back into place, and mended the sails while the cook cleaned his cauldron and pans.

Until nightfall, I shivered and huddled with the girls on deck under the blankets the sailors had given us. Then the crewmen unfurled the sails, and we headed for shore. I was certain that all of my clan prayed for my spirit and for my safe return to them or to my ancestors. Maybe I would find my father or Manu or even Kwesi here. I tried to be brave.

Before we stepped off the ship, a crewman gave us hard leather shoes. They looked as if they would torture my feet, as I was used to wearing soft, goatskin sandals. At first I shook my head, refusing them, but the moment my bare feet touched the icy gangplank, I put them on. The cold seeped through every inch of my body.

The captain and several sailors led all of us, including Tim and Joseph, down the narrow, cobblestone streets. One of the sailors carried a lantern, and I nervously stepped away from the frightening shadows of the square wooden buildings that lined the streets. Joseph saw the fear in my eyes and patted me on the shoulders, saying "good," which meant do not worry. The men hurried us along. They took quick glances over their shoulders, as if they were trying to hide something. I wished that Joseph could speak Ashanti so that he could tell me what was happening.

We entered a large, wooden structure, and I immediately smelled the scent of horses. I looked around and saw a row of stalls with horses behind them. Did people in this place keep animals inside their homes? I studied the wooden walls and dirt floor covered with hay and wondered what kind of home this was. Where were the brightly colored rugs to sit on and baskets to put clothing in? How could people sleep in the same smelly room with animals?

The girls were taken away by one of the crewmen. The man who had let us into the building left and returned with buckets of water. The captain seemed nervous as he spoke with the crewman who had remained with us. Then he said something to Joseph and left. We cleaned ourselves and put on the heavy coarse shirts, jackets, and trousers that everyone else wore. I thought of my beautiful robe and nearly cried. These clothes were much too large for me and the rough cloth made my skin itch, but I was able to slip my flute into a jacket pocket.

A black man, whom I had noticed in the room before, walked toward us with shiny metal blades and cut our hair. He had smooth black skin and a round face, reminding me of the goldsmith from my village, so I spoke to him in Ashanti. "Where am I? What's going to happen to me? Do you know? Are you in my clan?"

He stared at me, and I could tell by his blank eyes that he didn't understand a word I said. I wondered how he could appear so much like someone from my own village, yet not know Ashanti or Fanti. Joseph said something to him in the white man's language, and the man smiled at me, nodding in my direction.

The same man who had cut our hair brought clean hay, motioned for us to sit down, and gave us some watery soup. We sat on piles of hay where I promptly fell asleep. When I awoke, the girls were sitting with us, dressed in strange, dark-colored clothing, and the captain had returned with a man who was exceedingly tall and stout. I feared this mound of flesh with its intense pale eyes staring at us. I had been bought and sold enough by now to understand what was happening. The captain was selling us to this trader. He checked all of us except Timothy. I was too weak to fight or bite when he looked inside my mouth and squeezed my arms.

The captain and the trader haggled, shouting and gesticulating; they reminded me of the market women in my village. The captain got redder and redder. I thought his veins would pop out of his temples each time the trader spoke.

Finally, when their business was completed, I was relieved to find out that Joseph and Tim and I would remain together.

When the captain walked toward the door, Joseph trembled and his smooth, brown face was drawn and tired. For the first time since I'd know him he seemed afraid.

Tim's eyes darted all about as if he would spring and run at any moment. As I watched the captain walk away from us, I realized that we had all been sold to this wall of a man. We left the building soon after the captain.

The merchant led us to a horse and wagon. I trembled as I stared at the strange and frightening sights before me. It was light out, but I saw no sunshine. The sky and sea were the same smoky gray color, and the trees were bare. Their branches reached like the long skinny arms of a beggar to the sunless sky.

I looked around, foolishly hoping I might find my father and Manu waiting for me. But I saw no faces that I knew or loved. The little wooden houses and shops and shadowy alleys appeared ugly to me. I wanted to see the red clay walls of my family compound and the green trees that offered us fruit and shade and beauty.

We were still near the wharf, and I tried to see the ship that had brought us here, but I could not find it.

I noticed, however, that crowds were beginning to fill the street and ships were pulling in. I saw a few people with faces like my own, but they were dressed in the same drab, heavy clothing as the whites. The white women were the saddest of all. Their hair was not adorned with cowrie shells or braids; they wore no jewelry, only heavy, joyless clothing that was as drab as their world.

We soon left the narrow streets. Joseph and Tim and the rest of us rode in the cold, on the back of a cart pulled by horses. The trader rode in a carriage, which I, in my ignorance, thought was a tiny house pulled by horses. As we traveled through this foreign countryside, I saw nothing that resembled anything I'd ever known. This was a dead world, with no brightly colored flowers or robes. I willed myself to see my family's faces.

I saw a woman walking down the road carrying a basket, and I wondered why she didn't carry it on her head — as any sensible person would. Gradually, her white face faded, and I thought that I saw my mother's face. I breathed heavily and quickly, feeling as if I would choke. I saw their faces everywhere: Afua, Kwesi, Intim, and even Ama. I could see so clearly her eyes like two black moons. I shut my eyes as sweat poured down my face, even though I was very cold.

We stopped at a large, white structure, so different from our homes where one side was left open to the courtyard. I noticed that Tim was very quiet and seemed agitated as we entered. Joseph could hardly walk, his body racked by a hacking cough he'd caught aboard the ship. I was surprised when we entered a large room with shiny wooden floors. A fire burned in the huge fireplace and the room smelled of spices, reminding me of the herbs my mother burned to sweeten our home. I expected to smell animals and see horses inside the home.

The ticking clock and the images of men on the walls frightened me, though. Were these masks of spirits? Why were the images staring at me? Six white men and one white woman in a black dress sat behind a long table. Joseph saw the fear in my eyes. Even though he was weak, he put his arm around my shoulder while Timothy, standing on the other side of Joseph, held him up. The merchant led us before these unsmiling faces, and I knew that we were to be sold or traded once more.

Joseph coughed continually, and each time the merchant fired a stern look at him. We stood in the middle of the room, and some of the girls cried softly. One of the men, a tall, thin fellow with a long, sallow face, got up from the table and walked over to me. He immediately opened my mouth and I bit down hard on his hand. The man began to beat me about the head, but the trader stopped him immediately. Then he shook me himself.

The tall man walked away from me and examined the girls. The woman who'd been staring intently at all of us rose from her seat and inspected a particular girl who had not stopped crying since we left the ship. Protectively, the eldest girl put her arms around her narrow, heaving shoulders to comfort her.

No one looked at me, Joseph, or Tim. It was obvious that Joseph was sick, and maybe, since Tim was one of them, they could tell what his condition was by merely observing him.

Quickly, a man purchased the girls and took them away, and Tim, Joseph, and I were all who remained from the ship. The woman and a black-haired man with an oblong face and sharp lines running down the sides of his mouth stared at Tim and me and then spoke to the trader. Joseph looked as if he were about to cry, and I realized that we were going to be separated. Joseph and Tim both started talking at once and seemed to be pleading with the trader. I wished that I knew what they were saying.

The trader motioned toward Joseph. The man shook his head no. The woman walked over to me and thrust her face in mine. And though I still had not gotten used to the whiteness of the faces around me, I saw a glint of sympathy in her eyes, which, except for Tim, I hadn't seen in any of the other whites I'd met so far. Unfortunately, I could not understand her words. She looked from me to Joseph and kept repeating what sounded like "brother?"

I looked at Joseph, and he nodded, repeating the same word. So I nodded, too, stuttering "Bro . . . bro . . . brother!" and trying vehemently to say the word.

The woman spoke at length to the trader and the man with the lined face, who seemed to be arguing with her. She appeared to be pleading with him to take the three of us. I'd decided that if we were separated, I'd raise such a fury that they'd leave us all behind.

The man, the woman, and the trader turned their backs to us while they talked. My mind raced with fearful thoughts of what might happen to me next.

Finally, the couple motioned for the three of us to follow them. And as we followed, I was seized by a sudden jolt of terror. I had not crossed to the other side, to the place where our spirits went when we passed from this world. I would not see my father or any of my other ancestors. I had been taken across the seas far from all I knew and loved, to the land of the white foreigners who would try to make me a slave. I was kidnapped — a captive.

As we left the trader's house, and headed for where my new life would begin, a heavy sadness filled my heart.

XII
A Strange New World

We followed the couple toward another one of those small houses that was on wheels and tied to horses.

This time we were allowed to ride inside while the man and woman, driving the horses, rode on the outside. Though it was a very comfortable way to travel, I was distracted by my thoughts.

I studied Joseph's and Tim's faces as they stared out of the window. They did not seem the least bit disturbed, but talked quietly as they observed the countryside. I wished they knew my language or I knew theirs so that they could explain this new world to me.

How foolish I was, I lamented bitterly as we rode; I should have patiently waited for Atta to take me home. I should have told him that his son had taken my flute. I should not have convinced Ama to run away with me. And Kwesi is still waiting. I thought about my goldweight. Regrets are vain. There was nothing I could do about what had already happened. I had to look forward, not backward.

I had to learn how to survive in this place and to find a new way home. The sun didn't rise in this world I was in, but the sea on which we had traveled was the same sea that could take me back to my family.

We stopped at a large, grayish-white wooden building surrounded by smaller structures in the distance. I couldn't see much in the disappearing daylight. The cold air stung my face as we walked up the steps and entered yet another house.

We walked into a room similar to the room in the first house we'd been in. I was relieved that it was not filled with animals and didn't smell of horses. As I stood in the cold, gloomy room so thick with shadows that I could not see what lay in the corners, I longed for the red clay walls and the warmth of my mother's sitting room. The walls and floors of this room were made from wooden planks, reminiscent of the slave ship. The only bright spot was the red-and-yellow flames of the fire burning in the fireplace.

I was exhausted, and Joseph and Tim looked as if they would collapse from weariness also. The man and his wife both towered over us like two trees. The man spoke to us, and I, of course, barely understood a word. Tim and Joseph nodded their heads. The man left us, disappearing into another room of the house and his wife smiled at us slightly as she led us into a small passageway and then into a tiny room.

She pulled out bedding from a corner, and Tim and Joseph made three pallets on the cold floor. The woman spoke a few words and then left. We shivered as we took off our clothing and hung it on hooks. I felt inside my jacket to make sure the flute was still there. I then collapsed under the covers, too exhausted and hungry to worry about what would happen next.

The following morning Joseph shook me awake. I slipped out from under the blankets and jumped like a frog when my feet touched the cold planks. I quickly put on the rough trousers and jacket and made sure that my flute was in the pocket. As we rolled up our bedding, I was startled by the sound of a gong ringing five times and a girl's voice calling out. Tim and Joseph understood what things meant. We left the room and entered the narrow passageway. Joseph opened a door that led outside. It was dark and cold as I followed them to a little shed so that we could relieve ourselves. "Outhouse," Joseph said, pointing to the small structure made of wooden planks. I heard a rooster crowing as we raced back to the house.

We walked into the same large, shadowy room that we'd entered the day before. The man standing behind a chair, stared sternly at us. His wife sat in the chair next to his. She spoke to us, and I followed Joseph and Timothy to the other end of the table. As I gazed around the room, I noticed a very small and pale young woman who dished out food from an iron cauldron that hung over the fire. This was probably the couple's daughter. She looked very different from them, for they were both so tall.

As we sat down, there was a knock on the door. The girl opened it, and five men in rough clothing shuffled into the room. I thought at first they were the man's sons.

They bowed respectfully to the man and woman, but I wondered why sons wouldn't smile at their father or kiss their mother when they entered the home. I also saw that their clothing was dirty and their hands scarred and soiled. Would they possibly eat with such filthy hands? They paid no attention to me, Joseph, or Tim as they sat at the end of the table with us.

I noticed, as the girl placed two large bowls of porridge at each end of the table, that they cooked and ate in the same room. The girl also sat with us. I wondered why she didn't sit with her mother and father. And where were the man's other wives?

As the man began to speak, all bowed their heads. What was he saying? I sat straight up and stared at the tops of everyone's heads — including Joseph's. Joseph peeked at me and motioned for me to lower my head, too. I pretended that I didn't understand him. What was I bowing to? I saw no Ashanti king with a golden stool.

They raised their heads and ate in silence. Joseph and Tim gobbled down their food. Though I was starving, I stared at my plate. I had had to live like an animal on the ship, but now that I was living in a home again, I refused to be unclean. I motioned to Joseph, indicating that I wanted to wash my hands. Joseph shook his head and whispered, "Eat!" in Fanti.

As I stared miserably at my plate, Joseph spoke to the man, I suppose telling him what I wanted. The man yelled at me for not eating, then yelled at the girl who immediately picked up my plate and scraped the porridge back into the large serving bowl.

Joseph and Tim gazed at me with sorrow, but I would not eat again without washing, even though my stomach growled pitifully from hunger.

Occasionally, the other men would look up from their food for a moment, but then continue eating in silence.

After the meal, the five men left the room. Only the man remained there with us, and our instruction began. He talked to us at great length, with Joseph nodding all the while and taking nervous glances at me. I stared into the man's mouth, fascinated by the yellowish cast of his teeth and the odd sounds of his meaningless speech.

When the man finished talking, the woman entered the room with a broom and thrust it into my hands. I knew what she wanted me to do, but I feigned ignorance. This was woman's work.

Joseph then took the broom from her and swept, demonstrating to me what a broom was for — which I already knew. That was how the servants cleaned our courtyard.

I watched him, coughing as he swept. I was neither a servant nor a slave and would not be made to do that kind of work. The man snatched the broom from Joseph and shoved it into my hands. He then left the room, taking Joseph and Tim with him. I remained in the middle of the floor holding the broom. The wife bent down and peered into my face, saying what, I did not know. I stared into her mouth curious to see whether her teeth were as yellow as her husband's, but I could not see them. I then spoke to her in Ashanti.

"I am the son of a great important chief. I was taken captive and brought here. If you return me to my family, you will be greatly rewarded."

Her mouth became a gaping hole, and she backed away from me. Remembering how my father used to stand when he had meetings with the lesser chiefs, I let the broom fall to the floor and folded my arms and stiffened my back.

The woman spoke to me as if I knew what she was saying, but I stood there, determined not to give in, while she prattled on. What kind of foolish woman was this who talked to people who couldn't understand her?

It wasn't long before Tim and Joseph returned, bending to the weight of the logs they carried in their arms and stacked by the fireplace. I had not moved and still stood with folded arms; the broom lying by my feet like a defeated enemy.

Suddenly, as the man came in behind Tim and Joseph, the woman rushed over to him, shouting angrily and pointing at me.

Joseph's eyes became fearful as the man spoke harshly to me. And with a move so bold, even I was taken aback, Joseph stepped between us, picked up the broom, and started to sweep. The man pushed Joseph aside and shouted at him.

I couldn't understand their words, but I knew that Joseph was trying to protect me and was going to sweep for me. Suddenly I felt guilty. Because of me, he might be punished and beaten. No, I thought. I cannot let this happen to my friend.

I picked up the broom and began to sweep.

The man stopped shouting at Joseph. The girl put on a heavy outer garment that covered her from head to foot, picked up a basket, and left. Joseph and Tim also left once again with the man. I continued to sweep.

As I swept, the woman came to me and smiled kindly. She then pointed to the object I was sweeping with. "Broom," she said.

"Broom," I repeated pleasantly, straining to hold back my anger. Perhaps the white man's language would be useful in helping me to find my freedom.

She pointed to other objects in the room, telling me their names: "Churn, spinning wheel, table, pantry, plates, cups, spoon."

I repeated the words and remembered them. Gazing around the room, I pointed to various objects, and she told me what they were. I noticed for the first time a space in the wooden walls, and from this space I could see the cold, naked, gray trees and the gray sky. "Window," the woman said.

"Window," I repeated.

She showed me how to pound spices, and I was reminded of the way our cook pounded meal in almost the same fashion. I enjoyed the fragrant smell of the spices as I worked. She remembered that I hadn't eaten and offered me bread. I was almost faint from hunger, but I rubbed my hands together, indicating that I wanted to wash them.

The girl returned from outside, her face rosy with cold and her basket filled with eggs. She took off her heavy garment and hung it from a wooden peg. The woman said something to the girl, and she led me to a bucket of water in the passageway where I washed my hands and face. Then I hungrily ate every crumb of the bread she gave me, thanking her in Ashanti.

I spent the rest of the day in the house with the girl and the woman, learning how to chop vegetables, make tea, set the table, and do many other chores. I was not at all happy doing servant's work, but I had to be a strong man, like my father and brothers, enduring this slave's life until I could escape to my old life. In my heart, however, I was no slave.

When it was time for the evening meal, I put the plates on the table. Tim and Joseph looked exhausted when they entered the room with the man. They carried more wood and put it by the fireplace.

As everyone sat down at the table, the man bowed his head and talked for a long time, ending his speech by saying, "Amen." I remembered that word from the morning meal.

Again, I wondered as I ate, where the rest of this clan was. Surely this man had more children than one pale daughter. Where were his other wives and children? Why didn't they come to his home to bring food and eat with their husband and father? Surely he must have other wives, for he didn't appear to be a poor man. If he were poor, how could he have bought us? And where were the elders of this clan?

I gazed across the table. The man and the

woman ate without talking. I fought back tears as I thought about my own mother and the way we used to eat together in the sun-warmed evenings in her sitting room that was open to the courtyard. After meals, the whole clan would gather around my father's house as one of the elders told a story or I played my flute as Afua sang.

The room was chilly. I took a sip of the hot tea. Was it the custom of these people not to talk or laugh or sing?

After we ate, the girl indicated that I should remove the articles from the table. She filled a basin with water and showed me how to clean the plates and spoons. The man's wife sewed squares on to a large covering with many different squares while watching the girl and me clean. Tim and Joseph helped us. They both seemed as if they were near collapse. Maybe the man's clan would come later and would play some music. I felt the flute rubbing against my side. I ached to play my music.

When the room was clean, the woman put down her sewing. She walked over to the fireplace, fell to her knees, and clasped her hands. At first I thought that she was ill, but her husband didn't help her and the girl then fell to her knees in the same manner and also clasped her hands. Joseph and Tim did the same thing. I was the only one except for the man left standing.

"Kofi." Joseph motioned for me to join them. What were they going to do? Was this going to be a punishment?

"Good, good," Joseph said, smiling at me.

I walked over to them and kneeled. The man stood with his arms outstretched over our heads. He threw his lined face up in the air. Who was he talking to? Was he calling on his ancestors? Why was everyone on their knees with their hands clasped in front of their faces? We stayed in this position for what seemed to be a long time, and my legs and feet began to tingle as numbness crept up my side. Suddenly I heard a loud thud. Timothy had fallen asleep and fell flat on his face.

The girl covered her mouth, trying not to laugh out loud. Joseph had a fit of coughing. "Amen," the man muttered, then flew in a rage, beating Timothy about his head and back.

As everyone stood up, I glanced out of the window and noticed tiny white petals falling from the sky. Everything was covered in a blanket of whiteness.

"This is why these people are so pale," I called out to Joseph in Ashanti. "If that white matter touches us, will we not be pale, too?"

Joseph got up off his knees and looked to see what I was so excited about. "Good, good," he assured me. "Snow."

I cried out in fear, not understanding what Joseph had said, and in turn, the man shouted at me, which only made me more upset.

"I want to leave," I shouted in Ashanti. "I want to go home."

The man's face turned as red as a berry, and he gave me a good cuff behind my ear.

I stumbled to the room where we slept, and Joseph and Tim followed.

Pulling the scratchy gray blanket over my face, I vowed that no matter how long it took, I would leave that house and return to my own country.

XIII
A New Home

The first sound I heard the next morning was a rooster crowing, and for a moment, I thought that I was in my own village. But when the gong rang out five times, I remembered where I was.

Joseph and Tim also woke up. They talked softly as they put on their clothing.

I dressed hurriedly, for the room was freezing. We left the tiny room and entered the narrow passageway that led outside. When we reached the door, I hesitated, remembering the white matter from the night before.

"Good," Joseph tried to assure me, but when Tim opened the door into the morning darkness and I saw the ground and the trees covered with snow, I shook my head and refused to step outside. "Good, good," Joseph repeated. "Snow."

I shook my head. Tim left and went to the outhouse. Joseph tried to pull me, but I jerked away from him. Joseph shrugged his shoulders and left also. I stood trembling in front of the opened door. I waited, staring out into the white darkness, expecting Joseph to be as white as Tim when he returned.

I saw them racing across the ground as they returned to the house. Tim scooped up the white matter, made a ball, and threw it at Joseph's head. Joseph also picked up a handful and flung it at Tim's back. They both stomped into the passageway laughing and rubbing their hands. Joseph had not turned white, so I took a chance and stepped carefully on the ground, nearly sinking to my knees. I was surprised at how soft and cold the matter was as I slipped and slid to the outhouse.

Tim and Joseph were putting away the bedding when I returned to the room. I suddenly wanted to play a song and make the sun appear and the cold go away. My flute rested against my side and I took it out of my pocket and put it to my mouth.

Tim and Joseph both reached for the flute, and Tim shook his head and drew his finger across his throat. Joseph motioned for me to put the flute back in my pocket. "No good," he said.

What kind of hateful place is this? No wonder there was no sun here — there was no music.

As I followed the boys through the house, Joseph told me the names of the man and the woman and the girl. "Master Browne, Mistress

Browne, and Margaret," he repeated several times while Tim imitated the mannerisms of each one.

When we entered the large room, I was relieved to see that Master Browne was not there. Margaret was making a fire, and when we entered, she spoke to me, pointing to the plates in the cupboard. I knew that she was telling me to place them on the table as I'd done the day before, but I pretended that I did not understand her. How could she give me orders? She was not the wife nor the mother, but a girl not much older than myself.

She spoke to Tim and Joseph and they tried to make me understand what I already knew. I folded my arms and appeared to be very interested as Tim carefully picked up a plate from the cupboard and put it on the table.

"Plate," he said. I stared at him blankly, as if I had no idea what to do. The girl kept chattering as she put a log on the fire and watched it burst into flame.

Mistress Browne entered the room, smiled at all of us, and then looked at me and pointed to the cupboard.

I walked over to the cupboard and set the plates as I'd done the day before. Everyone except Mistress Browne looked surprised because I followed her orders. When I learned how to speak their language I'd tell them that I, Kofi, did not take orders from children like myself.

Margaret made an ugly face at me when Mistress Browne turned her back to pour water into a cauldron and then into a basin that stood on a stand by the fireplace. "Kofi," she called my name and pointed to the water. It was nice to hear a woman's soft voice call my name. I pushed thoughts of my mother and my sister and my grandmother from my mind; otherwise I'd begin to cry. While I washed my hands, Master Browne entered bringing cold and shadows with him. Joseph and Tim sat at the end of the table and he spoke to them. I sat down, too.

Someone knocked on the door, and the girl opened it, letting in a blast of cold air. The same five men entered, covered from head to toe with scarves, heavy outer garments, and headdresses that practically hid their red faces. They hung up their clothing on hooks and nodded toward the man and woman and sat down with Tim, Joseph, and me.

The girl brought the food to the table and sat down, and I knew exactly what to expect. All heads were bowed except mine, and the man spoke. I waited impatiently for the magic word, "Amen," so that he would stop talking and we could eat.

When the meal was done, the men left and

Master Browne, Joseph, and Tim followed. The girl put on her headdress and a heavy outer garment and also left carrying a basket. Again, I wondered why people in this strange place didn't carry baskets on their heads as any sensible person would do.

Mistress Browne and I remained. She walked over to the fireplace and stirred the embers, adding a small piece of wood to strengthen the fire. But the room was still cold and shadowy. I picked up the plates and placed them in the tub so that I could clean them.

"Kofi," she called me and pointed to the same objects she'd told me the names of the day before.

I remembered all of their names. "Window, plates, cup, cupboard, pantry." Then I pointed to the window and said, "Snow."

She smiled and clasped her hands. "Very good."

As she showed me how to churn butter and pound spices, she taught me more words. She also showed me the other cold, bleak rooms in the house and demonstrated how to make the beds and dust the tables.

I worked all day with the woman and the girl, and by the time I looked out of the window and saw that the light outside was fading, I was convinced that this land was too evil for the sun. I was also convinced that the woman was not Master Browne's wife, but his servant, for no wife worked so long and hard. There should be other wives to share the duties, especially for a man who was as rich as Master Browne seemed to be.

When it turned completely dark outside, Master Browne returned with Tim and Joseph, and the light inside seemed to fade as he moved his bulky self through the room. He looked at me and then spoke to the woman. Tim and Joseph dragged themselves to the table.

I put the spoons and plates on the table, and we sat down. Of course the man bowed his head, and I waited for the "Amen." After the meal, I helped the girl clean. Joseph and Tim went back outside. As I swept near the warm fireplace, I wondered whether there would be a time when someone would tell stories or sing songs. But when Master Browne, Joseph, and Tim returned with armloads of wood, we all had to get on our knees while the man talked to his ancestors. I kept peeking at Tim, hoping that he wouldn't fall asleep and send the man in a rage, but my eyes felt like stones, too. Joseph kneeled on one side of Tim and I kneeled on the other side. Each time Tim began to sag, we pinched him in his waist and he'd wake with a start.

Finally, Master Browne said the magical "Amen," and we stood up. The three of us fell exhausted into our beds.

One dull day melted into the next. But after seven sunsets, the routine changed.

XIV
The Long House

Tim and Joseph seemed happier when we woke up that morning. I could tell we had slept later than usual, as the sun was higher in the sky. I went straight to the large room and began my chores. I set the plates and spoons on the table, but oddly the girl did not bring the usual porridge. She poured milk into the cups and placed the bread that had been baked the night before onto the table.

When we finished eating, I waited for Tim and Joseph to leave with Master Browne as usual, but they did not. Rising from the table, I began to pick up the plates and clean the bread crumbs, but Mistress stopped me, saying a new word: "Sabbath."

Following the others blindly, I put on my outer garments and left the house. Where were we going? Maybe we were going to be sold again. Perhaps we will be given back to the captain who sold us, and maybe I would be sent back to the coast where he had found me.

Master Browne waited for us outside, and we all walked along a different path that led away from the house. I could clearly see the other wooden buildings in this odd compound. Maybe the man's other wives and children lived here, I thought, as we walked through the icy, slippery snow. The world was so different from my green forests and red-walled compounds. I strode between Joseph and Tim while the couple walked with straight, stiff backs ahead of us. The girl strolled next to me.

Here and there I'd spot a house, like the one I now lived in, standing alone on an empty hillside. Where were the ships and the sea that had brought me to this land? I saw no place where I could run to and no way yet to find my home — especially when I couldn't speak to anyone. I pulled Joseph's sleeve.

"Joseph? Good?"

He nodded. "Good, good, Kofi."

I felt a little better. Tim seemed happy whispering to the girl, and Joseph was not afraid, so maybe I had nothing to fear either.

We came to a forest, and I was surprised to see green trees with thin, pointed leaves. Some of the trees were very fat and some very tall. The woods gave off a sweet scent and were so thick that I could barely see the sky. When we came to a clearing, I was again surprised to see that we were in a place that looked like the area where the ship first left us, but there were no ships and no sea. Little wooden structures sat side by side but no one was going in or out of them. One long house, however, stood in the center of the compound, and many people were walking toward it and going inside. No one was riding horses nor was anyone riding in the little houses pulled by horses.

Everyone seemed to wear the same plain, drab, heavy clothing. We entered the long wooden structure, and I wondered whether animals were also housed inside. I was surprised to see that there were no tables for eating and no fireplace, but only rows of benches on either side of the room where people sat. This must be Master Browne's clan, I thought.

Mistress pointed to benches in the rear and motioned for us to sit. Margaret sat with us while Master and Mistress Browne walked to the front and sat down. As more people strolled in, I thought that all of the children would sit in the rear, the way we did at our ceremony, where the children and women remained on the outskirts of the arena. But some children and many of the women sat in the front.

A woman limped in slowly, grasping a stick. She sat on the same bench with us next to Joseph, and though I knew it was rude to stare, I couldn't help it, for her smooth black skin with few wrinkles and small, bright brown eyes reminded me so much of my own grandmother. I was embarrassed when she caught me looking at her, but she nodded her head slightly and turned her attention to the front of the room. How I wanted to speak with her. Where did she live? Where had she come from? Was she a captive like me? Could she speak Ashanti — or at least Fanti?

Suddenly a tall man stepped onto a platform. His hair was thick and white and seemed to fly in all directions. His white eyebrows stretched like a bushy tail across his forehead. As he stretched his long arms, everyone stood up. I remained seated, but Tim snatched my arm and pulled me up.

I stuck my elbow in Tim's stomach for grabbing me as if I were a piece of cloth, but I sensed that this was a special place and the old man standing before us was an elder. Elders had to be shown respect, so I remained standing. Perhaps he was going to recount the history of this clan. He stretched his arms as if he could touch each of us, and I knew that once he threw his head back as Master did, there would be much talk.

I lowered my head like everyone else, but my eyes were wide open as I peered around the room. There were two chairs on the platform, and the scene before me reminded me of our annual ceremony where our king and queen sat in front of us with the golden stool held over their heads.

When the man said, "Amen," I thought that we would eat. Instead, he lowered his arms and everyone sat down again; then he continued to talk. I looked at Tim who covered his mouth, stifling a yawn. Joseph's head was bowed, and I wondered why he didn't sit up straight like everyone else. Suddenly, a loud, uncontrollable snore burst from his mouth, and Tim hit him on the shoulder. A girl giggled and the man's eyes swept the room, passing over us.

As I listened to the drone of his voice, I thought of my last days before I was taken captive, and I prayed to my ancestors and the sky god Nyame to return me to my home. After sitting and hearing the man's voice for a very long time, everyone stood up to leave. I leaned over Joseph and spoke to the wonderful old woman I'd seen earlier.

"Mother," I said to her in Ashanti, "I am Ashanti, son of the *Amanhene*, Kwame, and I am being held captive here."

Her thin mouth opened slightly, and she stared at me. I thought that I had offended her in some way. But then her eyes seemed to melt like wax, and she embraced me and began to speak in Ashanti. "Mother, village, market, cloth," she said.

"Oh, mother, I am so happy to find you. Can you help me? I want to return to my village," I said excitedly. At last I'd found someone who understood.

She then repeated the same Ashanti words,

"mother, village, market, cloth," and smiled and said something else to me but in the white man's language.

Joseph spoke to her, and she shook her head sadly and touched my face with hands as soft as the finest cloth. I realized then that she'd said to me the only Ashanti words she knew. I wanted to follow her when she limped away from us. Where did she learn those words? Was she Ashanti, too?

As we stepped into the frigid air, I watched her small, lonely figure walk along the narrow path that led up a slight hill. While we walked home, I fixed in my mind the route we took and promised that I would return to this place and find her.

When we reached the house, we all went to the eating room. The dirty plates were still piled by the bucket and though I was happy that I didn't have to clean them, I wondered why they were to remain dirty.

Mistress gathered me, Joseph, Tim, and Margaret around the table while Master Browne went into another room. She spoke to us for a long time while I tried to understand as many words as I could. Then she turned to me and held up an object and pointed to it. "Bible," she said to me. She opened it and spoke again. Then she handed it to Joseph, who also stared at it while speaking at length. Margaret did the same. Tim also looked at it, but seemed to stumble and falter in his speech.

When Master Browne walked into the room, we all had to fall to our knees while he spoke on and on. It felt as if a season had passed by the time he had finished. When he finally said, "Amen," the gong rang five times, and we ate bread and drank tea.

I wondered what this new routine meant. I hoped that we would go to the long house the next day, too, so that I could see the old woman. But the following morning we went back to our usual chores. I worked all day in the house with Mistress Browne and Margaret. Mistress taught me more words, and I gathered them up like the Ashanti kings gathered gold.

I counted seven sunsets before we once again went back to the long house. I saw the old woman and spoke to her in the new language. "Good morning," I said, and she embraced me and repeated, "Good morning, child." Then her eyes seemed to tear and she repeated in Ashanti, "Mother, village, market, cloth."

Attending this place, I realized, was something that occurred regularly, and it was the only day there was no work — not even cooking. I looked forward to returning, for I'd see the old woman. However, several days after visiting the long house, Master Browne and Tim walked into the keeping room as I set the table for dinner. Joseph was not with them.

"Joseph!" I shouted, wondering what Master Browne had done to him.

Tim tried to calm me. "Joseph good," he said.

"Where's Joseph?" I shouted in Ashanti.

Master Browne glared at me and pushed me into the chair. I fell silent because I didn't want to be hit. There was nothing I could do or say to help myself or Joseph because in everyone's eyes we were slaves — Master Browne's property. I stared at my plate, and for some strange reason, I began to think of Oppong. I understood him now. Though my father treated him like a son and not the way Master Browne treated me, Oppong probably hated being a slave. Oppong was wrong to betray Kwame, but one human being could never own another.

And now, Joseph was gone, because he was merely a piece of property that Master Browne had probably sold.

XV
Secret Lessons

Salem, Massachusetts
April 1789

I flinched each time Tim hacked the tree trunk with the axe.

"You must say a prayer to the tree's spirit before you cut it down," I warned.

"Aw, mate, you know I don't believe in none of that nonsense. You're as silly as Master with his demons and devils."

"Not silly. One day your arm will fall off. We pray to the spirit, and then we cut the tree."

"I liked you better before you learned English." He lifted the axe. "You couldn't give advice then."

He whacked the tree trunk, and I smiled to myself as I raked the stones that Mistress needed for her garden.

Besides learning English, I had learned many things in the time spent in the home of Elizabeth and Jonathan Browne. I learned that Joseph was not sold elsewhere but was hired out by Master Browne to work for the baker. Joseph left early in the morning and returned in the evening when the clock rang ten times.

I learned that the men who ate breakfast with us every morning were not Master's sons, but farmhands who worked for him. The most surprising thing I learned was that Master Browne had only one wife, Mistress, and no children. Margaret was a servant. Her time of servitude was over, and when I knew how to do all of her chores, she was free to leave the Brownes and start a new life.

I covered my eyes and looked at the position of the sun. It seemed as if it were nearing noon. A crash startled me. The small maple tree Tim had been chopping down fell, and he stood before it wiping the sweat from his forehead.

"Tim, Kofi," Mistress called us from the steps of the house.

"Oh, no," Tim shook his head. "It's time for those bloody lessons."

I left the sack half filled with stones and quickly walked toward the house. Tim lagged behind. As I neared one of the many dead trees with thick bare branches, I noticed something different about it. Slight smells of living earth surrounded it — and it seemed to be coming back to life. Tiny round buds had formed on its branches, and a small brown bird with a red breast sat on one branch. I had never seen a pretty bird here. Perhaps the glorious bird's song was making some magical thing happen to the dead tree. Tim caught up with me. "What're you looking after?" he asked.

I touched one of the buds, and the bird flew away. "The dead tree is being born again."

"The bloody trees will bloom soon," Tim said. "It's spring."

Tim confused me sometimes — I had no idea what he was talking about.

Mistress Browne stood at the front door. "Come along, children," she said as we followed her into the keeping room. I was learning the language and the meaning of the symbols and signs that she called letters. We sat down at the table where we usually ate, and Mistress gave each of us a slate and chalk and I wrote the letters of the alphabet.

Mistress clasped her hands as if she were praying as she peered over my shoulder.

"Wonderful, Kofi. I'm amazed at how fast you learn."

I liked forming the letters. They reminded me of the markings the priests made on the temple for Nyame in my village. While I practiced, Mistress helped Tim; he knew his letters, but he had trouble when he combined them to make words.

Mistress's face changed from white to a bright red by the time she finished showing Tim the words and letters. Tim scratched his head and fidgeted and got as red as Mistress.

When the clock struck once the lesson was usually over. Tim practically leaped from the table. But Mistress put her long, bony hand on his shoulder. "Wait, you haven't read these words to me yet."

"But, Mistress, Master wants me to deliver wood to Farmer Edwards."

"That can wait. I don't want you to have a wooden head. You practice those words so you can read them."

She came over to me. "Now, Kofi, when you say your words don't pronounce them the way Tim does. He's not speaking correct English, you know."

Tim's head shot up out of his book. "But, Mistress, everyone understands me."

Suddenly the door opened and Jonathan Browne entered. He stared angrily at Tim. "You were supposed to deliver the wood. You haven't even finished splitting it."

"I just wanted to complete today's lesson," Mistress said.

"This is not a school, and you're no longer a teacher." He took a cup from the mantel. "You're ruining them. I told you God has a plan for each of us. The African is supposed to be a servant and is too dull to learn much, and people the

131

likes of Tim never learn more than to recognize and spell their own names."

I wondered what an African was.

Mistress gathered up the books and slates. "The black boy amazes me. He is very apt and learns so fast," she said showing him my slate.

He did not glance at it. "No more of these lessons. This is our busiest time."

She silently put the books and slates in the cupboard drawer. I felt sorry for her, for I could see that she enjoyed giving us lessons. Tim went to the door and made a face at Browne's stiff back.

I started to follow Tim, but Browne called me. "Fix me a cup of tea," he ordered.

He sat at the table like a great shadow. He had stopped the lessons, but he couldn't stop me from learning the language, and he couldn't stop me from figuring out how to return to my home.

The next morning, after I completed my chores inside, I started to go outside to feed the chickens and milk the cows and goats. Tim and Master Browne had already left.

I opened the door, but Mistress called me back.

"Wait, Kofi, sit over here near the chest." She sat me on the floor, hidden from view; as she glanced over her shoulder, she cautiously removed the slate and chalk from the cupboard.

"If Master comes in," she whispered, "slip everything in the chest and pour water as if you're brewing tea for me."

The lesson was short because I had to do my chores, but I was pleased that she would still teach me the words and letters, for I secretly loved the lessons.

When we were finished, I ran outside and headed for the chicken coop. I felt almost like my old happy self because I knew that if Mistress was willing to continue to teach me, she was my friend and could help me get back to my home.

As I passed the well, I noticed that the sun was very bright. Instead of going to the chickens, I raced to the outhouse and took my flute out of my pocket. I faced the sun and for the first time since my captivity I played a song — a song to the sun that had finally found me. Every morning when I awoke, I went to the outhouse, faced the deep pink ribbon in the sky, and played a song to the sun — and to Ama whom I'd not forgotten.

Each day grew warmer, and suddenly, from swollen buds, green leaves and blossoms burst. What stories I would have to tell Afua and the rest of my family when I returned.

Words grew on my tongue like the green leaves on the trees. I had a new language to put my feelings in. Master Browne did not find out about our secret lessons. Every Sabbath we went to church as usual, and I saw the old grandmother.

She'd always smile sweetly when we entered the church and bid me goodbye when she left.

One Sunday as I waved goodbye to her and watched her walk up the path, I turned to Joseph and Tim. "Where does she live?" I asked.

"I don't now," Joseph said. "Probably in the black settlement."

"What is that?"

Tim put his arm around my shoulders. "Listen, mate, it's like a village where all the old Africans who're no longer slaves live."

The Brownes were already walking away from us. "Was the old grandmother a slave?" I asked.

"I suppose so," Joseph said. "A long time ago."

"In this black settlement, she's free?"

"Yes," Tim said.

"I want to visit her. Can we go there?"

Tim's eyes sparkled. "Sure, mate. When the old windbag's away."

Joseph stopped talking. "You two better be careful. You'll get a good cuffing from Browne if he catches you roaming around and not working."

"You've lost your spirit, Joseph. Cuffing is good for you, makes your hide tough," teased Tim.

The days grew increasingly warmer and brighter, but Master was always around, for there was more work than ever.

Once in a while I snuck away from my chores and rode with Tim to the farms where he had to deliver wood or straw. Tim, however, visited the village where the old woman lived. "Her name is Jewel," he said. "And she makes the best fish-cakes in New England."

Master still tortured us with his long prayers in the evening, and Tim and I both had to be careful not to fall asleep while he was praying — otherwise we'd get a thrashing. We envied Joseph who was with the baker most of the day. Tim and I would lie on our bedding and try to wait for Joseph to come home in the evening. But most of the time we'd fall asleep before he arrived.

Tim would always say to him, "You're lucky to be with the baker. At least he doesn't work you like a mule."

"I wish I could work for myself," he'd answer. "All of my earnings go to Browne."

I thought that the days of bright sun and flowers would last forever, but slowly there was another change. The air turned sharp as needles, but the trees then changed to the most glorious reds, yellows, and oranges, like the beautiful robe my father had given me.

I felt that something terrible was about to happen, however. And I was right. For soon the leaves began to fall from the trees. Their branches slowly changed back to beggars' arms. Every day I watched the beautiful world fade. No matter how hard or long I played my flute in the dark mornings, the sun did not appear in a streak of light as before. And one dreadful morning as I fed the chickens, snow fell and the world died again.

XVI
Plans

Salem, Massachusetts
January 1790

The spring and summer months had passed so quickly that I never got the chance to visit the old grandmother. Cold days and nights lingered on, and no matter how much wood we put on the fire, the biting chill remained in the air. Home seemed farther away than ever, but I never gave up hope.

One snowy morning, as I sat behind the door writing on my slate, I asked Mistress, "Will the days be warm and green again?"

"Oh, yes, the flowers and trees will bloom once more," she answered. "The Lord giveth and the Lord taketh away. Every year there is winter — and then there is spring." She looked at me thoughtfully. "You seem so sad these days. I thought that you liked our lessons and were beginning to be happy here with us."

I had many words on my tongue and understood even more of the language than I could speak. I'd never talked to Mistress about my unhappiness before. Perhaps she was willing to help me. "I like the lessons very much, Mistress, but I am very homesick and must return to my home."

"But that's not possible, Kofi." Her eyes were soft and kind. "My child, you are too young to understand. By the grace of God you were taken out of the jungle so that your heathen soul could be saved. This is your home now."

"Jungle, Mistress?"

"Yes. Where you're from."

"I don't know what is jungle. I am Ashanti and was held captive. I am not a slave."

Her faced showed no understanding.

"Mistress, I am a captive here. My father was the great *Amanhene*, Kwame, a great chief. Our slave Oppong betrayed us and killed Father and my brother. I was stolen from my home, and my family doesn't know where I am. Can you please tell Master to send me home?"

She sighed. "You don't understand. You must accept your life here. It's God's will. I am going to pray for your soul." She turned away from me and looked out of the window. "Now read the sentence you learned yesterday, Kofi."

"*My book and heart/shall never part*," I read in the primer. Then I put the book and slate in the chest.

"Mistress, I don't want to read anymore. I'll do my chores."

She kept her back to me. "I know you're upset, but you must bend to the will of God."

I didn't know what she was talking about, but I did understand that she would not help me. She was not my friend as I'd thought. I could never accept living as a slave for the rest of my life.

During my chores, I thought of nothing except my disappointment. I was so sure that once I told her my story, Mistress would send me back to my home. Tim was always talking about running away, especially when he was angry with Master Browne. Maybe I, Tim, and Joseph could run away together. At least we would not be slaves to Master Browne. And I could find the sea again, to return me to my home.

That night, I left the candle burning and sat on the side of my bedding. "Tim," I whispered. "I must leave. I can't accept living as a slave anymore."

He rolled over on his pallet. "What? I thought you liked it here. The way you sit under Mistress and sop up them lessons."

"I like the lessons, but I am not a slave. I must return to my family."

He leaned toward me. "I thinks about leavin' all the time. Browne will work me to the death before my time with him is done." He sat up. "We could go to New York or Boston, you know, big cities where no one can find us."

The clock struck ten and a few minutes after, Joseph walked into the room. He rubbed his hands together as he shivered from the cold. "What're you two doing up?"

Tim pulled Joseph's arm. "How would you like to run away — to Boston or New York?"

Joseph scoffed as he began to take off his clothes. "That's silly talk. Tim, you only have a few more years to work for Browne, then you'll be free. You'll even get money and can begin a new life. Are you going to throw it away because you have no patience. If you run, you'll be put on the whipping post and jailed."

"Browne won't pay me my money," Tim replied bitterly. "He'll find a reason not to."

"And me?" I asked Joseph. "I will be free in some years?"

"You and I are slaves, Kofi. We belong to Browne for life."

My temples throbbed and I pointed to myself. "I am no slave. I am Ashanti."

Tim stopped rubbing his arm, which was always sore from chopping wood. "The old windbag thinks you're a black African slave."

"Kofi, someday we both might be free. Sometimes black people buy their freedom. There is a black man who works for the baker. He saved enough money and bought his own freedom from his master." Joseph pulled his bedding out of the corner. "Go to sleep now before you wake Browne," he mumbled.

But Tim was full of talk. "How could you buy your freedom from the windbag? He doesn't let you keep any of the money you make."

Joseph motioned for us to come close to him. "The baker gives me a few cents to keep for myself when he's very busy and I do extra work. He told me not to tell Master about the extra money. That's mine to keep, he said." Joseph reached under his blanket and pulled out a small purse. "See, I'm saving every bit of it."

"Aw, mate, Browne will never sell you back to yourself. He'll free you when you're old and useless, like the poor old blokes in the black settlement. I know his type. He gives away nothing."

"But you know what else?" Joseph's voice was barely audible. "Master Browne told the baker that me and Kofi were his servants."

That means," Tim piped in, "he ain't supposed to be buying African blokes here in Massachusetts, so he's telling people that you and Kofi is indentured like me. Still, he'll never free you, even though he ain't supposed to own you."

Tim turned to me. "You know, Kofi, he really didn't want me or Joseph. He purchased you, got Joseph here for nothing since the merchant wanted to get rid of him 'cause he was looking sickly and coughing something awful. He talked the merchant into givin' him my contract for less than what the merchant paid the captain for it. Mistress convinced him to take Joseph, 'cause she thought you two blokes was brothers."

Tim, always ready to clown, slid out of his bedding and imitated Mistress Browne as she stood over me. " 'Husband, these children have become attached to each other. The white boy is big and strong. He can help you chop trees and deliver wood.' "

Then Tim imitated Jonathan Browne's deep voice.

" 'I don't like these bound servants. They're difficult and lazy and they run away.' "

" 'But, husband, these are poor children,' " his voice squeaked like a little pig and we giggled.

"So," Timothy continued, "old windbag listened to his wife and now here we are."

"When the snow thaws and spring comes, I'm leaving. Will you blokes come with me?"

"I want to leave now," I said. "I will go to the black settlement where the grandmother lives."

He shook his head. "No. It's too close by. That's the first place Browne would look for us. And we can't run in winter. If we don't find shelter, we'll die of cold."

I blew out the candle. "So when the trees come alive, we'll leave," I stated.

"Both of you are foolish," Joseph whispered hoarsely in the dark. "You'll be a free man in four years, Tim, and can start a new life right here in Massachusetts."

"Can't wait that bloody long."

"We're leaving when the trees come back to life," I said. "You must come with us, Joseph."

"You both will regret running away," Joseph said, his eyes filled with fear. "You'll only end up with a worse master."

XVII
Decisions

Salem, Massachusetts
March 1790

By the end of March, the sun grew warmer and the days grew longer. One afternoon as I spread the feed on the ground and the chickens scrambled around my feet, the rattling of the horse-drawn cart caught my attention.

"Eh, Kofi, leave the chickens and come along with me to deliver this wood. The windbag has gone to Lynn."

I jumped on the cart, alongside Timothy. I knew Mistress would think I was milking and not look for me for a while. She no longer gave me lessons, except on Sundays when we'd read the Bible. She was still kind to me, but it seemed as if my telling her I wanted to go home disturbed her. I wondered whether she'd told her husband, but I couldn't tell, for his actions to me were just the same. I was only there to work and behave myself.

"Kofi, it's God's will that you be saved. That's why He sent you here," she'd reminded me again and again.

It was not God, but Sharif, who sent me here, I'd say to myself. Timothy knew his way around the village. As we rode along I played my flute as loudly as I wished. We traveled down a path lined with the bare trees. The sky was very blue, however, and the air was no longer frigid. Tim and I could begin to make real plans to leave. Spring was on its way.

Timothy dropped off a load of wood at a nearby farm, and I expected him to turn around, but he rode the horse straight ahead.

"Aren't we going back?" I asked.

"I want to make one more stop. Don't worry. I'll get you back before Mistress misses you."

We rode to the inn that was on the same road that led to the church. Tim tied up the horse, and we walked around to the back. A girl with thick pumpkin-colored hair threw out a bucket of dirty water as she greeted Tim. "Morning, Tim. Early today."

"Any customers yet?"

"A few, but I don't know as they want to hear you singin' and see you cloggin' so early."

I had no idea what was happening, but I was happy to be away from the farm.

Timothy put his arm around her. "Wait for me out here," he said to me.

I stood by the door and peered in as Timothy entered with the girl. The room was crowded with tables and had a large fireplace.

Tim took off his dirty woolen cap, stood in the middle of the floor, and began to sing. I couldn't catch all of the words, but the slow rhythm made it feel like a sad song to me.

Several men sat at a table and ignored him at first. But Tim had a loud, clear voice that finally captured their attention; they asked him to sing another and another. When he finished, the men threw coins at him. He bowed, picked up his money, gave the girl a coin, and we left.

"See, that's how I makes me a little extra money, Kofi. And selling a few pieces of Master's wood." He laughed and rubbed his arm.

"You're stealing Browne's wood?" I asked.

His eyes gleamed. "I don't call it stealing. Just taking what windbag don't pay me for. It's business, you know. Sometimes I cut a small tree that even Master don't miss. Then I sell it cheap to the old blokes in the black settlement." He looked up at the blue, cloudless sky as we rode toward the farm. "Spring is coming. I can smell it."

He pulled at the reins of the horse. "You know, I just had an idea. I could teach you my songs, and you can play them on your flute. You could make money for yourself, too." He grinned. "Kofi, me and you and Joseph can go to Boston in style."

When we reached the wooden gate that led to the house, I spotted Mistress heading toward the barn, and I knew she was looking for me. I jumped off the cart and raced toward the out-house — the next place I knew she'd search when she didn't find me in the barn.

I stayed there waiting for her to knock. "Kofi, the cows are about to burst."

"Oh, Mistress," I whined. "I've been sick. Stomach hurts. I had to come here."

"You have stomach pains?"

"Oh, yes, Mistress, but they're better now since I relieved myself."

"Well, hurry up now. There's plenty to do."

I did my work with a light heart. Soon, I would no longer be a captive.

A few days later, I snuck away to the inn with Tim again. I had no fear of Mistress looking for me this time because she'd sent me to gather stones.

Timothy made a delivery and then we went to the inn. On the way he asked, "Can you play for me?"

"Sing once, and I'll listen."

He sang and I caught the tune and played for him. It was a slow song with a sweet melody. In between the pauses as he sang, I added my own notes from the music I had played in my country.

Since it was near noon, the inn was crowded with men — drinking and talking loudly. I was reminded of my voyage on the slaver, and I didn't want to enter. But Tim pushed me in.

The people threw coins at us when we were

done. Then Timothy did the stomping, jumping dance I'd seen him do on the ship, and the memory of the time came back to me. I followed his rhythm and played for him as the crowd threw more coins at us.

Timothy and I laughed as we left the inn, our pockets full of coins. "We're rich men now, ain't we lad?"

"We'll buy windbag's farm," I joked.

"Yes, give him that same bloody strap he likes to lay on us," Timothy said swinging his arm as if he were whipping someone with a strap.

I remembered what Kwesi had told me. "We do not repay evil with evil," I said.

Tim started to say something to me, but as we rode away from the inn and down the lane we saw Farmer Edwards.

"Oh, just our bloody luck, Kofi. I hope he didn't see us leaving the inn."

"He didn't," I said and thought no more of it. I played on my flute as we rode back to the farm, enjoying my little piece of stolen freedom.

At dinner that evening Browne recited grace as usual and we ate in silence. Joseph returned to the farm early that evening. The baker, to whom he was hired out, entered the kitchen with him. At first I thought that Joseph had done something wrong.

"He is a good worker, but I'm closing my business and won't be needing his services." He gave Browne some coins and left.

"You'll work on the farm until I can hire you out again," he told Joseph. "Have you eaten?"

Joseph nodded.

"Fill the water barrel and put water in the basins." Joseph smiled at us weakly and left the room.

"Hope windbag doesn't pray us to the death tonight. I want us to talk," Timothy whispered to me as we ate.

I cleaned the kitchen as usual when we finished eating. "You can go to bed when you're done," Mistress said.

I was relieved — we would be free from the long nightly prayer.

When I entered our tiny bedroom, I heard a knock on the front door. I wondered who it was since the Brownes rarely had visitors. Joseph and Tim were already lying on their pallets, talking as quietly as possible.

"Kofi, Tim was telling me you went out with him today, but you best be careful. If you make Browne angry, he'll get rid of you both."

"I'm gettin' rid of myself. Me and Kofi's leaving. You should come with us."

"Yes, Joseph," I repeated. "Come with us."

Joseph shook his head. "I'm not running anywhere. You'll regret it if you leave, Kofi, when you're sold to a worse place than this — to the southern states or to Cuba. You can't do what Tim does!" he said angrily.

"Why?"

"Because you're a black slave and Tim is white."

"I'm Ashanti! And Tim is a white slave!"

"Wait a minute, mate, I . . ."

"Shush! Both of you. I don't feel like a whipping tonight."

Tim frowned. "We could go to Boston or New York," he whispered.

"We can't go with you. It's easy for you to run. You're white. That's why these New Englanders prefer having slaves. You bound servants can always get away and blend in with everyone else," Joseph crossed his arms.

"I'm tellin' you, mate, Boston is a big city and New York is even bigger. When we get there, no one will find us."

"They might not find you, Tim," Joseph said solemnly. "Even if we reached as far as Boston, someone is bound to ask to see Kofi's and my certificates."

"You're losing all the spirit you once had," Tim said.

"There is a law. All people of African descent must have a certificate from the government saying they can live in Massachusetts."

"Do they have this bloody law in New York?"

"But we will be stopped *here*."

"We'll leave at night, and if we're stopped, I'll say you belong to me."

I chuckled at the idea of us belonging to Tim.

"You're ridiculous," Joseph said. "What kind of gentlemen would you be, with those rough leggings and wild hair and smelling like a horse? How could you own slaves?"

"Maybe he could clean up and dress like a gentleman," I suggested.

"It's a foolish idea. If we go to Boston or New York, all me and Kofi could do is be stable boys. We'd be worse off than we are now. I've been to both places, and I've seen how the free blacks suffer. Yes, it might be good for Timothy to run. If he cleans himself and gets some good clothing on his raggedy hide, he might indeed become a gentleman one day. We never can, Kofi."

Joseph's eyes watered as the thoughts he always kept inside poured out. "For us, Kofi, running means only poverty and hunger if we're not caught, and if we are, we could be jailed and sold again."

I wasn't certain anymore what I should do — stay with Joseph or go with Tim. Had I been patient in the past, I would still be in my own country, but as my goldweight said, it was useless to regret the past. If I waited, like Joseph, I might be a slave forever. I started to speak when the door to our room burst open and the chill that always followed Browne filled the room.

He snatched Timothy off his pallet. "You and that little black devil were dancing and playing in the inn."

"No, sir, we were not inside the inn."

"You're a lying rascal. Farmer Edwards saw you and him leaving." He pointed a long accusing finger at me.

"Sneaking to that inn!" he thundered as he beat Tim.

He then turned his wrath on me, but I picked up the candlestick. I heard Joseph yell, "Kofi, no!" as he knocked it out of my hand. Browne covered me with blows, but I refused to cry. Timothy's face was on fire. "Sir, we only stopped at the back of the inn for a drink of water. Me throat was dry, sir, from the dust we kicked up in the road."

He brought the strap over my chest and shoulders, and it felt as if a million red ants were stinging me. Browne struck me again and again as the clock rang ten times. I finally screamed.

"Quiet!" he ordered. I curled into a ball and whimpered as he beat Timothy again.

"The good farmer inquired about your business there. You've been regular tramps. Singing and dancing and who knows what other sins you've committed in that place. Where's that flute the African was playing?"

My mind raced like a hunted rabbit. "I have no flute," I said.

"T'was an old vagabond what let him play on his flute," Tim helped. I heard Joseph wheezing heavily in the dark silence. Suddenly he pulled Timothy and me off our pallets. "Get in the kitchen," he ordered.

We stumbled to the kitchen, followed by the long shadows his candle threw. "On your knees," he ordered.

We sank down to our knees before the dark, cold fireplace. He stood over us, arm upraised, holding the candle in one hand. The shadows made me wonder whether I was in a real world or a spirit world.

The candlelight shining on his long, white face made Browne look like one of the masks used to frighten away evil spirits.

"God, bring your light to bear on these two heathens. Save them from eternal hell and damnation. Take the demon out of the African's black soul."

I wondered what a heathen was. My body ached from the beatings, and I wished he would let us go to sleep. Instead he tortured us with a long prayer. When the clock rang twelve times I heard loud snoring next to me. Timothy had fallen asleep, which put Browne in a new rage.

He beat us both again and sent us mercifully to bed. But I was happy, for now I had no more doubts as to whether I would leave or stay with Joseph.

Our punishment was not over. I woke up before anyone else, and the first thing I did was hide the flute in the cupboard. When everyone came in the kitchen for breakfast, I served them. As Tim started to sit, Browne pulled him away from the seat. "Kneel in front of the fireplace. Kofi, when you're finished serving us, you join him. I tried to pray for you both," he said. "Now you better pray for your own salvation."

He made us kneel all morning. Joseph did my chores, but whenever Mistress left the room he'd sneak us a piece of bread. When she went to milk the cows, she turned to Joseph. "If you let them get up or give them food you will receive the same punishment."

I was surprised; I had expected her to be sympathetic. She gazed at both of us. "How could you boys repay our kindness this way?" Tears welled up in her soft, brown eyes. "God blessed you, Kofi, with a good brain and you, Tim, with a strong back. This is how you repay Him? Not to mention my husband and all he has done for you both."

She left, but I had no idea what she was telling me. I was the one who had been wronged.

Joseph bowed respectfully. "Yes, Mistress." He remained by the open door. "It's safe now, boys, she's heading for the barn. We stood up on aching legs. "I'm leavin' tonight," Tim announced. "I'll not be tortured another day."

"I'm leaving, too," I said.

Timothy danced a stiff, defiant little jig. "Get some life back in me legs."

I imitated his stomps. My feet felt as if sharp needles were sticking me. Tim and I laughed and danced in Browne's house of gloom. Joseph looked nervously outside. "If you two would stop defying him, you wouldn't get beaten," he said.

"That's easy for you to say. You haven't been with him all the time," Tim said, dancing harder.

I could only think of one thing. "Let's leave when the clock strikes twelve," I said, as I poured myself and Tim two cups of cider. I felt good in spite of my sore legs. Joseph continued to stare outside. "You'll regret it, Kofi."

"I must leave," I said, sorry that my friend did not understand my feelings.

"The whole time Browne was praying, I was making me a plan in me head," Tim grinned.

"Until you fell asleep and crashed to the floor," I laughed.

Joseph started to cough and wheeze.

"She's coming boys. Get back down." He closed the door and nervously glanced at the cups and the cider to make sure everything was in place. Mistress came back carrying two pails of milk, and Joseph immediately took the pitchers off the mantel.

Master Browne entered behind her and ordered us to stand. "I have hired you out to Farmer Edwards," he said to Joseph. He then turned to me and Tim. "Go to your chores, and the next time you defy me I'll get rid of you both."

When I was finally alone, I took my flute out of the cupboard and returned it to my pocket. We worked very hard for the rest of the day, Tim and I acting as though we were sorry for our behavior. But we had decided to leave at midnight when we were sure that Master and Mistress were asleep. As we lay fully dressed in our pallets in the evening, waiting for the clock to ring twelve times, we tried to convince Joseph to go with us.

"Leave with us, Joseph," I pleaded.

"We're going to the black settlement," Tim said.

Joseph coughed and seemed to have trouble catching his breath. "That's the first place they'll look for us," he rasped.

"The old grandmother will help us," I interrupted.

"He's right," Tim said, "the people in the settlement help runaways. They'll hide us or sneak us out of Salem."

The clock struck twelve times. Tim pulled my arm. "Come on, mate. He doesn't want to go."

"Joseph, please."

"I'm not as brave as you and Tim," he said, his voice choking.

Tim pulled my arm again, but I couldn't leave my friend. "Joseph, it is better to be stable boy and free, than slave."

Tim pushed me toward the door. "I'm leavin' both of you if you don't come now!"

"We get caught, we just run again. As long as we have legs to run we are free. Me, you, Tim, we help each other," I explained.

To my great joy, Joseph finally sat up and put on his jacket.

XVIII
Runaways

We eased open the door in the passageway. It squeaked and we froze. Joseph wheezed nervously, and I hoped that he wasn't going to have one of his coughing spells. I pushed the door open, and it squeaked even louder. Tim and Joseph hesitated again. But I pushed it wide open and boldly dashed out, running like a bird before it takes flight. I was free.

Had Browne been looking out of his bedroom window, he would have seen us racing to the gate and down the road. At last I'd get to see where the old grandmother lived. Joseph and Tim led the way. The little village of leftover people wasn't really a village at all, but a collection of tiny log cabins sitting close together at the edge of a pine forest. Tim quickly took us to a small cabin as a dog barked in the distance. He tapped on the door. "Aunt Jewel, it's me, Tim."

She opened the door, and we stepped into a tiny room. Her bedding lay in one corner, and a table with a bench on either side sat in the middle of the cabin. "My God, children, what are you doing out so late?"

"We're running away from Browne, and we want to go to Boston," Tim said.

"That's a long way from here." She looked at me and Joseph. "I ran away from a cruel master once. But he found me and whipped me, and I ran away again, and he found me again, and . . ."

"Aunt Jewel," Tim interrupted her, "we have to get out of Salem before the sun rises."

"This is the first place he'll look when he finds you're missing."

Joseph pulled my sleeve. "That's what I was telling you. We'll get caught for sure," he said.

She motioned for us to sit down at her small table, and she sat across from us. "A lot of runaways pass through here. A man come last week, all the way from Maryland. Maybe my friend Lucas can help you. He told me yesterday that he was going to the election day celebrations in Lynn. His heart is as large as his hind parts," she laughed. "He's helped many a runaway."

Tim sprang off the bench and hugged her. "I knew you would help us," he exclaimed.

She smiled and waved him away. "Don't thank me yet. Let me see what old Lucas says first. Heat up some water for tea." She got up stiffly, threw her shawl over her shoulders, and shuffled to the door.

Tim, who knew his way around the tiny cabin, took the kettle off the fireplace.

"Suppose this man can't help us. What then?" Joseph asked with a worried look on his narrow face.

"Someone will help us," Tim said. "I have a lot of friends here."

We jumped at every creaky sound as we waited for Aunt Jewel to return. Finally, she walked into the cabin, and a short, round bubble of a man carrying a fiddle followed her.

"Hello, Tim, Aunty tells me you and your friends want to get to Boston."

"Yes, can you take us?" Tim asked nervously.

"I'll take you as far as Lynn. It's election day celebration time." He held up his fiddle. "Have to play my music and make a few coins."

"It's a big celebration?" Tim asked.

"Yes, people come from miles around to play games, dance, and have fun. If they like your music, you can make a lot of money."

I saw the gold coins gleaming in Tim's green eyes.

"Master Browne goes to Lynn," I reminded him.

"Yeah, but he just went a day ago. He won't be going back there anytime soon."

Tim stood up and pulled me off the bench. Joseph still looked worried as he too stood up.

"This is bloody good fortune, mates," Tim

grinned. "We could make us extra money singin' and playin' and hire a fine horse and carriage to take us to Boston."

"Let's get out of Salem," Joseph cautioned. "We'll worry about Boston later."

Aunt Jewel held my face in her dry, wrinkly hands. "You children come back here to me if you can't get to Boston or life is too hard." She then tousled Tim's wild, yellow hair and patted Joseph on his shoulder. "I will hide you until Farmer Browne gives up looking for you."

We bid Aunt Jewel goodbye and left the cabin. As we climbed into Lucas's wagon and hid comfortably under a pile of hay, I peeked out so I could take one last look at the little village of old people, freed from their lifelong bondage. I felt strong. I had left the house of my captivity, and I had the language of this country on my tongue, and I had Aunt Jewel to return to if I needed help.

"You boys stay hid, now," Lucas warned. "If I get caught carrying you away, I'll be going to the whipping post along with you."

The three of us fell into a deep sleep and did not wake up until we reached the town of Lynn, Massachusetts, that afternoon. I couldn't believe the sights we saw.

"Well, boys, here we are," Lucas announced. This was the first time I'd seen so many happy people in this country. Lucas explained the celebration to us. "The white men who have money and property vote for a new government to tax them and tell them what to do. The rest of us come to the big celebration after the election."

The three of us jumped off the wagon, which Lucas tied to a tree near the wharf where other carriages and horses also stood. "Let me show you where the fun is," Lucas said, swinging his fiddle and bouncing ahead of us.

Wiping the hay out of our hair and off our clothing, we followed him past shops and cobblestoned streets to a large market. Music rang through the sweet, spring air. I saw some women whose beautiful shawls reminded me of the Ashanti robes. "What people are those?" I asked Joseph and Tim.

"They're Indians," Lucas answered. "Always been here before the white man came."

Everybody came out for the election day celebration. People danced and sang together —poor whites like Tim, blacks, sailors, Indians, men, and women. The fiddling and singing and dancing reminded me of the great ceremonies of my home.

Black and Indian men and women sold meat, sweets, jewelry, carvings, shawls, bowls, baskets, and other things that they had made. The black women wore brightly colored headcloths and skirts, and the Indian women wore beads in their straight, black hair. My eyes opened as wide as the bright, blue sky, for I never thought that I would find so much color and life in this somber land. I was truly happy. Browne would never find us among so many people.

The people drank, danced, and played paw paw, a game Tim knew well from the ships.

"You throw four cowrie shells." Tim explained. "If three land with their faces up, you lose; if four land facing up, you win," he explained. "We can play after we make some money."

"You'll lose everything you make," Joseph warned. Lucas put his fiddle under his chin. "Okay, boys, let's see what we can do." Lucas played a song that Tim knew. He sang and I listened until I could catch the tune and join them. People began to gather around us and throw coins, which Joseph collected. I felt as if I were home. We played our music, ate fried fish, and drank cider. Tim drank rum, however, and the more he drank, the louder he sang.

We divided the money we'd made equally with Lucas, earning enough to pay a stable boy a half dollar to let us sleep in the stable where he worked.

"Well, boys," Lucas said, "we had a grand time. I'm going to bed down in the cart and head back to Salem soon as it's light."

"You're not staying another day?" Joseph asked.

"No. Got to get back home. But I've made

enough to buy some chicken feed and a few other things I need. I wish you boys luck and godspeed." He shook our hands and we thanked him.

The next morning we strolled over to the marketplace and bought sausage and coffee for our breakfast. Timothy held his head as we passed the harbor and found a spot under a shady maple tree. "Me head feels like it's comin' off."

"That's all the grog you drank," Joseph said. "I warned you." Joseph himself coughed a lot and seemed to have trouble breathing, but I felt refreshed and hopeful, and Tim was wild with excitement.

"We made five dollars yesterday. We have enough to buy new clothes and — "

"We need to get to Boston, remember?" Joseph, who was leaning against a tree, cut him off. "We could pay someone who has a horse and wagon, maybe, to carry us."

"The celebration's not over. We could stay one day longer and make some more money," Tim said.

"You know Master is searching all over for us by now," Joseph coughed nervously.

I took a sip of the rich, hot coffee and then handed it to Joseph. "Here, take a drink of coffee, and don't worry so much." The market was getting crowded. Soon the second day of festivities had begun. We had an even better time than the day before.

I was amazed at the spirited dancing of the people. They spun and twirled like colorful whirlpools. Everyone danced together — blacks, whites, Indians. I felt like the king of Ashanti as many coins were thrown at my feet and faces of all colors smiled in my direction. When I played my flute, I combined the rhythms and tones of my country with the new melodies I was hearing. I learned more tunes, and Tim danced and sang until he looked like a big, red carrot. And all the while, Joseph collected the money.

The crowd swelled around us as we made this great multitude swirl like a windstorm. I even did Tim's dance while I played. The crowd roared. Tim grinned from ear to ear as I danced along with him, matching his steps perfectly. The crowd cheered us along, and even Joseph was smiling as he swooped up the coins.

All of a sudden, Joseph's mouth flew open in surprise, and I felt an arm wrap itself around my neck and pull my head back.

XIX
The Captain

"Leave them alone!" someone in the crowd yelled while I struggled to free myself from the iron grip. Twisting myself around until I faced my attacker, I found myself staring into Master Browne's face. He also held tightly onto Tim with his other hand, while Joseph coughed and choked.

"These children belong to me," he bellowed.

"Let them go," someone shouted. I kicked Browne in his shins, and at the same time the crowd surged forward to rescue us.

"Why are you spoiling our fun?" A tall sailor with a bright red beard pulled Browne away from us as easily as if he were flicking a piece of lint from cloth.

I fell down, but I scrambled up and pushed my way through the multitude of people.

"Stop them!" Browne yelled.

"Go away," a woman shouted back at him.

I ran, taking a quick glance behind me. Joseph and Tim followed, while fighting broke out among some of the men. As we ran, a group of constables passed us, heading for the angry mass of people.

"Let's go back to the stables," Joseph rasped. "We can hide there." But as we left the alley and stepped back onto the street, we saw Browne in the distance, with the constables, heading in our direction.

If we tried to go to the stables, we'd run right into them. We turned around and flew in the opposite direction.

"Stop them," Browne shouted.

"Thieves," someone else yelled.

A sailor tried to grab us, but we were too fast for him. We clambered down the steps leading to the dock and before we could even think about what we were doing, we raced across the gangplank of a schooner. But suddenly I stopped short, remembering the horror of my all-too-recent experience on a ship. I was afraid to enter. Tim was stronger than I and pushed me onto the ship. Joseph was already on board and ran across the deck toward several barrels.

Memories of the slave ship enshrouded me in terror, and I tried to fight Tim, but he practically lifted me up and threw me behind the barrels.

"Shush!" Tim ordered. "We'll only be here a few hours, mates. We've just got to get away from Browne. We might be . . ."

Approaching footsteps suddenly quieted us.

Joseph's chest heaved up and down as he tried not to cough, but he couldn't stifle it. He coughed and the footsteps stopped.

"Who goes there?" a voice called out.

Sweat beaded up on Joseph's face as he tried not to cough again. Tim patted him on the back, and I wiped his face with my shirt sleeve. Joseph's eyes began to roll up in his head as he tried not to cough.

"Who's there?" the voice called out again.

Tim held his fingers to his lips, warning me not to answer as I listened to my heart pounding in my chest. We all remained as still as statues, but a sharp wind rocked the ship to one side, pitching the empty barrel that had been concealing us to the ground with a crash.

We must have looked like frightened puppies. Joseph hacked and coughed, no longer holding his breath.

"Come out at once," the man ordered.

I was surprised to see he was not a white man. He was stocky and had copper-colored skin and a round face with full lips and nose. His curly black hair shone in the sunlight spreading over the deck. His black suit was made of finely woven material. "What are you doing? It's a crime to stow away on a ship. Don't you know that?"

Joseph couldn't stop coughing, and I was too frightened to speak. Tim wrung his hands nervously. "We're not stowaways, sir. We're running from our cruel master." He looked suspiciously at the man.

"You are a bound servant then?"

"Yes," Tim answered.

The man stared at me. "And you? Why are you hiding on my ship?"

I told him my story also. Though his face was serious, I saw sympathy in his eyes.

He turned to Joseph next. "Are you a slave?"

Joseph, still coughing, nodded.

Maybe the man was a great and a good chief. I began to feel calm.

"It seems as if you were smuggled in on a slaver — the same as the girl I saved last year on a slaver bound for the West Indies." He put the barrel back in place. "I'll take you to the cook's galley. He'll make you tea and give you food. Then we'll see how we can help you."

I heard a commotion behind us and turned around quickly. A chill passed over me as Browne boarded the ship along with several guards and a constable.

"These children belong to me," he thundered at the kind man. He reached for Tim and the man jumped in front of all three of us, blocking Browne's grasping hand.

"They say that you have mistreated them and that they had to flee from your home."

"Please don't make us go with him," Tim begged.

"I am a captive," I cried.

The man turned to the constable. "This matter must be handled by the court," he said.

"What right have you to interfere?" Browne challenged the man. "These children belong to me and that settles the matter."

The red-faced constable stared at the man. "Where is your master? Who gives you the right to keep these children?"

"They were hiding on my ship. I am a free man, a citizen of this state. Captain Paul Cuffe is my name, and you're on *my* ship. I only want to help these children."

The constable looked shocked. "This is your ship?"

"Yes. I have my papers here." He reached inside the pocket of his jacket and pulled out several papers.

The constable glanced at them quickly and then returned them to Captain Cuffe.

"I don't believe him. He's probably the servant of the captain. This is a fine schooner," Browne said, fastening his eyes on every detail.

"I have papers, sir, to prove that I am who I say I am."

The constable nodded at Browne. "I don't think he's lying."

Several crewmen came on board. Two of them were black and one was an Indian.

"Captain, is there a problem?" one of the sailors asked.

"No. Everything is fine." They bowed slightly and went below deck.

"I suppose this is his ship," Browne muttered.

"These children must not be forced to go back to this gentleman unless their complaints are heard," Captain Cuffe said, slightly bowing toward Browne. "As a citizen of this state, I insist that the law be followed." He stared directly at the constable. "You know, sir, that it is illegal to import slaves into Massachusetts. Also, even though the children are servants or slaves, if they are abused by cruel masters, they have the right to petition the court for removal from the home."

Timothy began to shout. "Please, sir, please, Master Cuffe, don't make me go back to him." He pointed at Browne.

I joined Timothy, yelling also, while Joseph coughed.

"Quiet, everyone!" the constable ordered. "They have to go to prison until a judge decides what to do with them."

"We are not criminals," Tim declared.

The constable pushed the three of us between the two guards. "Captain, you can petition for their freedom, but Mr. Browne has claims on them. It's the law, and I have to take them to the prison house."

171

We left the boat and walked back, between the two guards and the constable, to the center of town. Captain Cuffe promised to help us and to remain in Lynn until we were freed.

As we walked along the dock, I could hear the celebrations. Life changes like the blink of an eye.

We were put in a small, foul-smelling cell in the prison house. Timothy and Joseph explained to me what a court and a judge were as we lay on a pile of hay on the floor.

"It's like elders and chiefs in my country," I said. "When I return home, the chiefs will punish those who kidnapped me."

"Kofi, you might never return home," Joseph said, "but if the captain helps us, we'll at least be free and get papers that allow us to live and work in Massachusetts."

Captain Cuffe visited us that evening, bringing bread, cheese, and milk along with blankets for us to sleep under.

"On Thursday morning, the judge will hear my petition on your behalf," he informed us. "And I have hired a lawyer who, like me, is very much against human bondage."

Tim, who had been unusually quiet, spoke up. "Why do you want to help us?"

"Son, my father was brought here from Africa and made a slave. When he became a free man, he married my mother who was from the Wampanoag — the native peoples who were here before the whites." He stared deeply at each of us. "I am a man who is the product of two despised races in this land — the Indian and the African. I hate slavery and mean to fight it whenever I can." He paused and seemed to be in deep thought for a moment. "I am a Quaker, and we are against slavery. We believe that God's light shines on us all. I have a girl who has been living with my family for a year. I saved her from a ship that was illegally smuggling slaves into Rhode Island."

Joseph, who always thought ahead, said, "Sir, if we're not made to go back to Browne, what work will we do?"

"You can work for me. I need apprentices to build my ships."

He lowered his head. "This slavery is a terrible thing. But one day, my ships will return all of those who want to go, back to their African homes."

I stared at him in disbelief. Could it be true that this kindly ship captain wasn't a slaver? Could he take me home? "Sir, sir, thanks you."

Timothy and Joseph laughed. "It's thank you, Kofi," Joseph corrected.

"Tomorrow will you take me home?"

"No, son, not tomorrow, but as soon as I am able."

I could not hide my disappointment, but as I thought of my impatience during the time I spent at Atta's — waiting for him to help me — I vowed I would wait until Captain Cuffe could bring me home and not try to leave on my own.

Each day seemed like a hundred seasons as we waited to go before the judge. Finally, Thursday morning came. Captain Cuffe arrived at the prison house with clean new clothes for all of us. I had a jacket and trousers fitted to my size. We left the prison house and were escorted by two guards and the constable to the courthouse where the judge would decide our fate.

It was only a short walk across a yard from the prison house to the courthouse. The election day celebrations were over, and the only music came from the birds in the blossoming trees. "See, it's a good thing we went to the ship," Tim said.

"That depends on what happens. The judge might make us go with Master Browne," Joseph sighed.

XX
The Hearing

We were led to the prisoner's bench in the front of the shadowy room, lit by shafts of light from the high, narrow windows. The benches, where a number of people sat, and the raised platform in front of the room reminded me of the meeting house. Captain Cuffe sat behind us while Jonathan Browne and Mistress sat stiffly on the benches to the far right of us. I was surprised to see so many people whom I did not know. I recognized, however, the big sailor with the red beard. A man in a long black robe entered the room and sat behind a table on the platform in front of us.

It was the first time I'd seen people here wearing robes. The elder in front of us, the judge, spoke a lot of words that I did not quite understand, and when Browne stood up to speak, a chill spread over the room.

"These boys are scamps," he said. "I took in the African and the other black boy. A merchant by the name of James Foster had them. My wife and I needed servants and farmhands. I know nothing of illegal slaves — I'm not a slave trader."

The judge looked over his small, round spectacles.

"Did you exchange money with the merchant?"

"Yes, sir."

"What did you think you were buying — cornmeal?"

"Sir, I went only to obtain an indentured servant boy because I needed a farmhand." He stared at Timothy. "The merchant let me buy out the white child's term of servitude. He's a big, strong boy, and I needed a laborer. I took in the two black boys out of the goodness of my heart. That one is sickly and of little use on a farm," he pointed at Joseph. "And the other one is a child. He was a little savage and had to be trained to do the simplest chore. I took him in because the three children had grown close, and I kept them together because I am humane. And this is how I'm repaid for my kindness. The white boy is of as low moral character as the two little black heathens."

Joseph coughed nervously. "He is a liar. Oh, what an evil man."

Timothy grew redder and redder before my eyes. Suddenly he shot up like a flame. "Sir, sir, the man is lying. I was there and know what was said!"

"Quiet, you." The constable grabbed Tim by his collar. The elder banged a mallet on the table. "Silence! Young man you will get your chance to speak," the judge shouted. He said something to the constable who pointed at Captain Cuffe.

"Captain Cuffe, come before this court," the judge ordered. "How did you meet these children?"

"They were hiding on my schooner — the *Sun Fish*."

"Are you petitioning the court for these children?"

"Yes. They say they've been mistreated. The African boy claims to be a captive." Captain Cuffe turned around and nodded in my direction. "Slavery is outlawed in this state. I'm willing to take the boys and train them in the arts of navigation and shipbuilding."

I looked at Captain Cuffe's broad, strong back and felt almost as if my own father were protecting me.

"I will also educate them to read and write and be useful citizens of this state."

"But what about the white child? He is a bound boy and Mr. Browne has paid for his services."

"I will give Mr. Browne back whatever money he has paid for the boy and take him also as my apprentice." Browne stared straight ahead as if he had nothing to do with the proceedings.

"Now, you may speak," the judge said, turning a stern face to Timothy.

Tim stood up quickly. "Sir, I was there when Master Browne purchased Kofi. He paid the merchant for my contract what the merchant got from Captain Stewart who smuggled the slaver into Boston. You see, the trip was a bust, sir. The ship was ruined in a storm and most of the slaves and crew died from small pox.

"Joseph was thrown in for nothing on account of the Mistress thought Joseph and the African were brothers and said it was inhuman to separate them. He didn't want no parts of Joseph 'cause he could see he was sicklylike. I was a bound servant to the captain on that slaver for four years."

"How old are you?"

"Fourteen. I was took on the ship when I was ten."

The judge cleared his throat. "Tell me, young man, had Captain Stewart previously smuggled slaves into New England?"

"Yes."

He called Joseph next.

"How did you come to be the captain's slave?"

"My mother died giving birth to me on a slaver."

The judge looked puzzled. "Who took care of you when you were a baby?"

"Sailors and crewmen, sir. One was very good to me. He taught me my letters and instructed me in the Bible."

"Are you a Christian?"

"Yes."

"How old are you?"

"Sixteen years, sir."

The judge looked at me next. "What is your name?"

"Kofi."

"Do you know your age?"

"Thirteen seasons."

"Seasons?"

"Years," I said, remembering that in this place time was not calculated by the seasons of rain, planting, and harvesting.

"How did you come to be with this man?" he asked, pointing to Browne.

I repeated my story as best I could in my new tongue.

"You were the son of a great chief and were illegally kidnapped?"

"Yes, sir!" I said. "And I want to go back to my home."

"But won't you be enslaved in your home? You are going back to a land of savages. Don't you think you're better off here?"

I had no idea what a savage was. "My people are Ashanti. If I am taken to my village, my mother and my clan will rejoice at my return."

Everyone was silent. The judge looked over his spectacles and addressed the people.

"This is a strange case, indeed. The African was smuggled into this state and sold illegally. Though the importation of slaves is outlawed in Massachusetts, smuggling occurs, and the poor unfortunates are sold to southern slavers."

He looked at Browne. "You, sir, could be fined eight hundred dollars for knowingly purchasing a slave in this state." He clasped and unclasped his hands. "There have been instances when the state has sold illegally imported slaves to the South and used the money to aid the poor of our own state. We could free the Africans into Captain Cuffe's custody and he will have the responsibility of providing for them."

I prayed to Nyame, my ancestors, and the god Mistress had taught me about that this elder called a judge, who seemed to have so much power, would let us leave with the good Captain Cuffe.

"The African claims to be freeborn, but the boy Joseph was born a slave. But how do we know that Joseph's mother wasn't also captured illegally?"

"May I address the court?" Captain Cuffe asked. "What is legal slavery? Slavery is against the highest law, God's law. I maintain, sir, that there is no such thing as legal slavery. That is a contradiction of terms."

"Your points are well taken, Captain. These boys are not citizens of this or any other state. The bound boy is a British citizen. If we find that he's been abused, then his contract can be broken and he'll be returned to Britain as a free citizen. Is that what you'd prefer?" he asked Timothy.

"Well, sir, I prefers to stay here, but not with Master Browne, sir. He beats us for breakfast, dinner, and supper."

"If this court finds that the gentleman mistreated you, then you can remain in this state as long as you find work and make yourself useful. I'm sure a big, strong fellow such as yourself will have no trouble finding work."

Browne stood up, and I wished that I had darts to shoot in his hindmost parts.

"Sir, may I speak?"

The judge nodded.

"That bound boy is a lazy scramp. If he is allowed to remain here, I know he'll do nothing but roam from one bawdy inn to the other singing songs in exchange for drinks. As for the other two" — he looked at Captain Cuffe — "you'll be sorry you took them in. See how they've repaid my kindness. You won't get a good day's work out of either one of them. They should be confiscated and sold and the money given to me and my dear wife for the food, clothing, shelter, and moral instruction I've given them for a year. And furthermore, the boy Timothy is a liar, or didn't understand what he saw and heard. I purchased his contract from the merchant. I did not purchase slaves."

Timothy shot out of his seat. "The man is a bloody liar," he shouted. "His wife knows that what I say is true."

"Young man, you'll be put out of this court," the judge warned.

"Tim, shut up. They'll think you are a scamp," Joseph whispered to him.

The judge called Mistress Browne. She walked stiffly to the front of the room, her face covered by her large, black bonnet.

"Did your husband knowingly buy slaves?" the judge asked her.

She lowered her head, and I prayed to my dead father's spirit to make her tell the truth as she had always told me to do.

"No, my husband did not knowingly buy slaves." She was barely audible.

"She's a liar!" Timothy shouted. "A bloody, bloody liar."

Tears streamed down his angry, red face. I stood up, too. "They buy me," I shouted, pointing to myself. "They buy us all."

Joseph coughed and hacked.

The judge banged his mallet on the table and stood up. "This hearing is adjourned!"

He left the room, and the constable and the jailer pulled us up out of our seats and pushed us toward the door.

Captain Cuffe followed us. "Boys, the judge will give you no sympathy if you carry on like that in court. Tim, he'll send you back with Mr. Browne, and Kofi and Joseph, he'll sell you to the southern slavers."

When we returned to the courthouse the next day, I listened closely to the judge as he addressed us. "There is no proof that Jonathan Browne knowingly purchased slaves. Since this is a free state, these two black children should not be held as slaves, nor, as Captain Cuffe has pointed out, should the state of Massachusetts be in the business of selling humans to the slave states. Mr. Browne says that he did not purchase the blacks, therefore they do not belong to him."

The judge looked over his glasses at Browne. "However, sir, if you are willing to pay them wages or indenture them for a term of seven years, they will be returned to your home and custody."

"I will not!" Browne thundered. "I have supported them for over a year! I should be paid!"

"Then," said the judge, "they are free to go with Captain Cuffe." Joseph and I practically jumped out of our seats.

"They are your responsibility," he addressed Captain Cuffe. "If they run away from you, then they shall be sold and sent away from this state."

He nodded in our direction. "You are free to go with Captain Cuffe."

Joseph, Tim, and I jumped up and hugged each other. People clapped and I pulled out my flute and began to play. The judge banged his mallet and shouted, "Order!" and we sat back down. The room was silent as he signaled Tim to stand up.

Timothy stood quietly with his hands behind his back and a serious look on his face. There was no play in him.

"As for the bound boy" — the judge peered over his spectacles once again — "it does not appear to me that you are abused. You look strong and well fed. You have a sturdy roof over your head and are being trained to be a useful citizen. You owe Jonathan Browne three more years of service."

Joseph and I both gasped. I knew that he would not stay more than a week with Browne before he ran off again. I felt sorry for Timothy and wished that he could come with us.

We left the courthouse with Captain Cuffe and waved sadly to Tim as he climbed into the Browne's carriage. His playful green eyes were like two full cups of water as he took one last look at us. We stood watching the carriage roll down the winding path, away from the court-house. We both missed Tim already. I hoped Browne wouldn't beat him too much, but I knew that Tim was in for a good cuffing.

"Come, boys, we have to leave now," Captain Cuffe said. "One of these days you'll see your friend again."

The town didn't seem like the same place now that the election day celebration was over. Everything was quiet, and the streets were empty as we walked to the dock.

Joseph and I stood on the deck of the *Sun Fish* watching the harbor disappear, and I wondered what to expect in yet one more new home.

XXI
A Face from the Past

Westport, Massachusetts
1790

It was still dark when the *Sun Fish* reached Westport. We took a short ride in Captain Cuffe's carriage to his farm. As we rode along the path leading to the white farmhouse, I saw the first glimpses of the rising sun, pointing the way to my real home. At least, I knew I was free. And of course, I could not have been more grateful for that.

Captain Cuffe jumped off the carriage and hurried toward a large white house that looked like the Browne's home. I stepped out of the carriage and stared at the light spreading from the east. I had a good feeling about this Captain Cuffe and did not for the first time in a long time fear the future.

The inside of his house bore no resemblance to the shadowy, somber rooms of the Browne home. We entered a large bright keeping room that was filled with the smell of coffee and spices. Captain Cuffe embraced a small woman with straight black hair. Like his mother, she was an

Indian woman. "This is my wife, Alice." Then nodding slightly toward us he said, "These two young men will be my new apprentices."

She smiled at us warmly and extended her hand. "Welcome to our home," she said.

The captain sat down at the table and motioned for us to join him. "What a time we've had in Lynn."

She prepared a breakfast of porridge and freshly baked bread as Captain Cuffe told the story of our meeting and the trial. When we finished eating she said, "Welcome to freedom. You have a new home and a new family now."

I thought Joseph would hop across the table, he was that excited, and so was I. "Thank you so much," he said. "Oh, thank you."

My spirit was peaceful as I also thanked them.

"You boys must be tired," the captain said as he led us up a flight of stairs to a good-sized bedroom with a fireplace, two small beds, and a dresser.

He sat on the bed next to me while I pulled off my shoes. "Sleep as long as you like. You'll meet the rest of the family later."

When the captain left, I said to Joseph, "I hope this isn't a dream and that we don't wake up in our room at the Brownes'."

Joseph folded his trousers on a chair. "It's no dream, Kofi. We are two lucky boys."

I slid under the soft, clean covers. "It's too bad that Tim couldn't come along with us."

"Don't worry, Tim can take care of himself." He climbed into the bed and sighed deeply. "Kofi, this is better than a dream. I have my freedom, a family, and a bed to sleep in all in the same day."

At least I had once had a real family of my own but poor Joseph had never even known his own mother. Suddenly I thought about Oppong for the first time in many months. He'd never known his own mother either. That was worse than any revenge I could ever have brought on him. "I am happy for us both, Joseph." I propped myself on my elbow. "I think we are safe here."

All I got for an answer was a loud snore. Joseph had fallen into a deep and peaceful sleep — and so did I. We woke up later that same day and, after throwing water on our faces from the basin on the dresser and putting on our clothes, we went downstairs.

"Listen to all of the talk and laughter," Joseph said. "This doesn't sound like Browne's home."

"I hear young children," I said. We entered the keeping room and the captain's little girls all chattered at once. Even the baby, who sat in its mother's lap, gurgled and cooed happily.

"Hello," one of the girls who was about seven seasons piped up. "My name is Naomi."

"And I'm Mary," another one shouted. She

was about five seasons. A third daughter, who was almost a baby herself, spoke to us in her own language.

Mistress Cuffe laughed. "What she is saying is that her name is Ruth and the baby's name is Alice."

Joseph sat next to her. "How old are you Ruth?" he asked.

She held up two tiny fingers.

"Naomi," Mistress Cuffe said, "call Phyllis so she can meet Joseph and Kofi." Mistress Cuffe stood up and put the baby in a large basket. "This is Phyllis's time to study her primer. She's learning how to read." She kissed the baby on the cheek. "Phyllis is the girl my husband rescued from a slaver."

"Your husband helps many people, doesn't he?" I asked.

"Yes. We are Quakers and we hate slavery." She closed her dark eyes and rocked the baby. "If he could, my husband would bring every fugitive from slavery to this house."

Naomi dashed into the keeping room and when she returned with Phyllis, I thought that I was again imagining the faces of loved ones. "Phyllis, meet Kofi and Joseph," Mistress Cuffe said.

Phyllis had eyes like two black moons. Though her slender frame wore the clothing of the whites, my eyes were drawn to a goldweight that hung from a ribbon around her neck — my father's goldweight.

"Ama?" I whispered.

"Kofi?"

The children, Joseph, and Mistress Cuffe gathered around us with curiosity, joining in our jubilation. We embraced, laughing and weeping at the same time. At first we were unable to speak for we were both filled with powerful emotions. When we found our voices, we spoke Ashanti to each other.

"You have a new name?" I asked her.

"Yes. I took a name in this language, but I am still Ama. See, I have not forgotten our language even though I've learned a new one."

"How did you get here?" I asked.

"I ran away from Sharif. I didn't want to marry his son, and you gave me hope that I could find my way home. Sharif found me again and sold me to Apo, the same man who had your brother."

"You saw Kwesi?"

"No. But one of the girls who was captured like me told me that a young man named Kwesi was the only one there who was not chained like an animal. A few days before I arrived, his brother had come to get him. All she talked about was the young, handsome Ashanti who came with servants and body guards to rescue his brother."

"That was my brother, Intim," I said. "Either

Apo or Atta got word to my family. They know then what happened." I closed my eyes and remembered all of my loved ones. I was truly at peace now. Kwesi was safe, and my clan knew that Father and Manu were dead, and that I had been taken captive.

"Apo sold me to a white man and I was put on a slaver and sent here. It was horrid. Many people died in the dark, stinking bottom of the ship. We were being smuggled in, and the authorities of this state seized the ship. Captain Cuffe found me crying and shaking among the other survivors. We were going to be sold in another part of this country, but Master Cuffe was allowed to bring me here to live with his family, Kofi, and they have treated me as if I were truly their daughter."

Mistress Cuffe interrupted our talk. "Are you brother and sister?"

"No," I answered, "but we are like brother and sister. Excuse me, Mistress, for speaking in our language. We didn't mean to be rude."

She motioned for all of us to sit. "I understand. When I am with my people we speak the language of our ancestors, too."

Ama, Joseph, and I told Mistress Cuffe and the older daughters our stories. "I prayed that I would see Ama again," I said when I finished recounting my tale.

"I prayed that I would see you again, too," she

replied, fingering the goldweight. "I remembered the lesson of the goldweight, and I don't think about what has already passed. These are good people, Kofi, and we will all be safe and happy here."

I thought about the lesson of the goldweight also. And as I gazed around the table at Mistress Cuffe, her daughters, Joseph, and Ama, I understood why regrets are in vain — they keep your mind and heart in a place that is no more and prevent you from living the life you have. I knew at that moment that I was truly a man.

Captain Cuffe entered the room and picked up the baby while Naomi and Mary swarmed around him, excitedly telling him that Ama and I had known each other in the past. As I watched him listening attentively to our story, I thought about my father. Captain Cuffe was, like Kwame, a great chief. I made a decision right then that I would be a great chief, too, as my father Kwame had been, and as my new father, Paul Cuffe was. I, too, would fight against slavery and open my home and my heart to unfortunate men and women in bondage. The trials of my life had not been in vain.

I had no more regrets.

Epilogue

We are so close to the shore that I can see the palm trees lining the beach. I also see what appears to be several ships that have been captured and condemned by the British, who have banned the slave trade in their territory. I am reminded of the time, 23 years ago, when I was rowed to the white man's water house. I am now piloting a water house.

As I look past the palm trees into an interior that I cannot see, I imagine the Ashanti village of my youth. But I will not try to find it. When I complete this voyage to Sierra Leone and we unload the cargo, I will return to Massachusetts, for that is my home now with my beloved wife, Ama, our children, and Joseph who is like a brother. Joseph, Ama, and I have dedicated our lives to helping fugitives who have escaped from slavery. And there is still much work to do. My Ashanti village lives only in my soul.

Author's Note

This story is purely fictional; however, it was inspired by "The Life of Olaudah Equiano, or Gustavus Vassa, the African," Vassa's true story of his life. I was fascinated by the narrative, written by a man who spent his early boyhood in Africa before he was kidnapped and sold into slavery. His tale makes the reader understand and feel what it was like to have been enslaved. It also reveals Vassa's intelligence, strength, and sensitivity and is part of a distinctly American literary form — the slave narrative — spawned by the African-American experience.

Kofi's trek to the coast, his fear and curiosity on the slave ship and when he enters a home in Boston, and Ama's description of the raid on her village are all based on Vassa's narrative.

Paul Cuffe was a real person. He was born in Massachusetts on January 7, 1759. His father, Kofi Slocum, was an African who was enslaved when he was about ten or eleven years old. He purchased his own freedom when he was about twenty-five and married Ruth Moses, a Native American.

Despite racism and restrictions against blacks, Paul Cuffe became a wealthy merchant and sea captain. With his crews, composed of men of Native American and African descent, he took flour, bread, grain, beef, and general merchandise to Africa, and transported and traded cargo in Massachusetts, Philadelphia, Delaware, Maryland, and the Caribbean. Cuffe was a religious man, a Quaker, who was against slavery. In 1811, he voyaged to Sierra Leone, on the west coast of Africa, in order to explore the possibilities of forming a colony of blacks from America who wished to return to Africa. Cuffe died in 1817 in Westport, Massachusetts. His dream of forming an African colony did not materialize.

The Ashanti empire flourished from the seventeenth to the early nineteenth century, in what is present-day Ghana and parts of the Ivory Coast and Togo. It was important to me also to show that Africans came to the "new world" bringing a rich cultural past with them.